DESIRE LINES

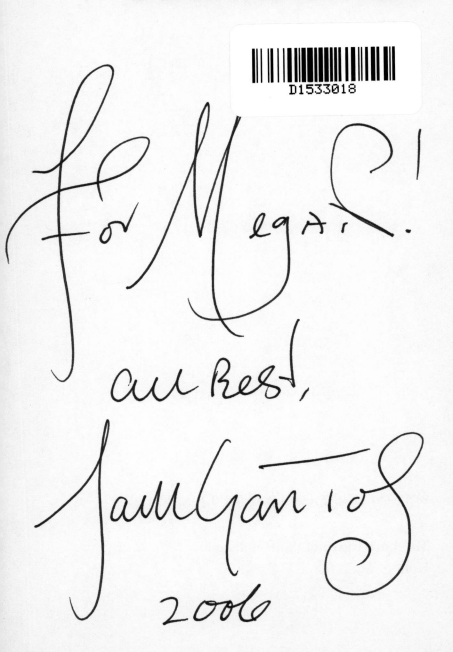

For Megan —

all Best,

[signature]

2006

DESIRE LINES

JACK GANTOS

Farrar, Straus and Giroux / New York

Copyright © 1997 by Jack Gantos
Published in Canada by Douglas & McIntyre Ltd.
Printed in the United States of America
First edition, 1997
Farrar, Straus and Giroux paperback edition, 2006
10 9 8 7 6 5 4 3 2 1

Library of Congress Cataloging-in-Publication Data

Gantos, Jack.
    Desire lines / Jack Gantos.— 1st ed.
        p. cm.
    Summary: When sixteen-year-old Walker gets caught up in a witch-hunt
against homosexuals, he is left to stand by and watch as a tragedy unfolds.
    ISBN-13: 978-0-374-41703-1 (pbk.)
    ISBN-10: 0-374-41703-2 (pbk.)
    [1. Courage—Fiction. 2. Lesbians—Fiction. 3. Prejudices—Fiction.] I. Title.
PZ7.G15334De   1997
    [Fic]—dc21

                                                        96-54707

For the one who lived
and the one who died
at the duck pond
on Peters Road

DESIRE LINES

In the Beginning

Florida, where I live, is mostly a soft limestone shelf attached, in the shape of a sock, to the lower end of Georgia. In the last few years it seems more and more sinkholes have suddenly opened up. One day your back yard is a solid plot of green grass, and the next day you have a bottomless pit filled with water. I expect, in the future, when people fly over the state they'll look down and find nothing but a rotting Swiss cheese slowly dissolving in the Gulf of Mexico. Just last week another hole opened up, this one under a Porsche dealership in OpaLocka, and about a dozen cars were sucked down into the pit as the ground gave out and the water slowly seeped in. Another opened under a house in Gainesville. Some people say Lake Okeechobee is nothing but an ancient sinkhole. You never know where they'll strike next.

Still, my sinkhole had to be the most beautiful. Mine had become a duck pond hidden in the middle of a golf course that was abandoned about twenty years ago. From what I could make out, the pond had been a tough water hazard worked into the joint of a dogleg on the eleventh hole. If I could ever have seen the bottom, if there was a bottom, I'd probably have found it covered with a heap of slimy old golf balls. It made me wonder what someone might find if they ever got to the bottom of what I was made of. Eventually, I found out for myself, but only after someone had died because of what I'd done. And then I wished a sinkhole would open up under me.

I used to spend a lot of time sitting around the mossy edge of the duck pond, reading and feeding stale bread to the ducks, thinking about nothing and everything and staring into the water, then lying back to feel the earth spin. The water was glassy and dark blue, not brackish like in the drainage canals, and so inky it was easy to imagine the nib of an enormous fountain pen dipping into the pond, refilling its barrel, and writing down this story.

Overhead was a canopy of oak branches, and when the wind blew, the shafts of light which sliced through the leaves shone deep into the water and crisscrossed like klieg lights searching for a criminal in the night. Every now and again a needle of light reflected off the scales of a shiner and it blinked like a big silver eye and darted off. In an odd way it made me think there was something festive going on under the surface, some exclusive club I couldn't join. Often I would lower the book I was reading onto my lap and just stare deep into the water, searching for a clue about what was down there. But after so much staring I'd drift into a stupor and feel myself almost hypnotized, the back of my brain slowly stirred with those shafts of light, and the eyes of the fish blinking like foreboding thoughts I couldn't quite turn into words. I had to give my head a real hard shake to snap out of it. Real hard. When I got all tensed up like that, walking without a destination was the best thing for me. I'd pull myself away from the pond and with each step I felt like a giant ball of string unwinding until I was nothing but a quiet trail.

In ancient city planning there was something called a desire line. This was a footpath created by people who wanted to get from one place to the next in the quickest possible time. In the book I read, ancient planners were praised because they understood that people liked to walk in a straight line from place to place. To me, they were simply using common sense.

But modern city planners don't seem to use common sense. For example, in my neat-and-tidy neighborhood, sidewalks always turn left or right at ninety-degree angles. But when you look at the ground, at any street corner, you see where people have strayed from the sidewalk to cut the corner and have trod a path diagonally across the grass. As anyone knows, the quickest way from point A to point B is a straight line, not a right angle. A desire line. I used to love that term. To me it meant you do just what you feel like doing in life, and it turns out to be a better way of doing things than what you have been conditioned to do. Living by desire, by your guts. Not living by the rules of some anti-desire city planner who designs gated communities and cul-de-sacs.

Personally, I had two as-the-crow-flies desire lines. The first one was from my bedroom, down the hall, halfway across the living room, onto and over the coffee table, out the front door, pivot a hard left across the front yard and down the street, cut through the Metrics' front yard, avoid their two-foot-high tempered-steel sprinkler heads, avoid the low-foreheaded Metrics altogether, then march a dotted line from yard to yard, block to block, across roads, over hedges, fences, and lawn furniture, paying no attention to the dirty looks I received for violating the sanctity of private property, until I arrived at Wilton Manors Boulevard. From there I tacked across the street, dipped through a hole in the chain-link fence which was directly beneath a NO TRESPASSING sign, and entered the southeast corner of the golf course. At that point I'd cut through the brush, penetrate the tree line, work my way to the pond and take a deep breath, and think, Free at last. Free at last. Thank God Almighty, free at last. I figured the Underground Railroad was the greatest American desire line ever built. The Trail of

Tears was the most shameful. Then I'd put on my ear-phones and listen to some jazz.

Jazz was my music of choice. Jazz definitely had great desire lines. It was without boundaries. It was all pas-sion. Freedom. Emotion. If you were to picture jazz it might look like the northern lights, or water swirling down a drain, or leaves blowing off a tree, or a glass ex-ploding as it hits the floor, or steam escaping a whistle. That's how jazz is. No matter if it is hot and spontaneous, or cool and totally controlled, it is always real. And when you hear it you close your eyes and go with it, follow it directly to a place where it rules.

My second desire line was from the classroom door of Mrs. German's English literature seminar, my last class of the day. Usually we just sat in her class and read. But I couldn't read there. For instance, when we were read-ing Edgar Allan Poe I should have felt all the twisted ro-mantic nature of his characters and stories. I should have had sensations that I couldn't even begin to put into words, like when the depraved guy in the poem "Annabel Lee" shacks up with his dead girlfriend at night "in her sepulchre there by the sea." I'd be right there with him until I lifted my eyes from the page and saw the dull yel-low walls, low ceiling, broken Seth Thomas clock, and the half-asleep Mrs. German. Then the entire life of the poem got bleached out of me. It was impossible to iden-

tify with a necrophiliac in that place, even though most
of the students around me were about as alive as cadav-
ers.

So I would sit in class and pretend to read. Every
three minutes I'd stifle a yawn and turn a page. Then, as
soon as the release bell sounded I'd bolt for the door. I'd
cut right, not toward the buses, but down the outdoor
passage and across the all-purpose gym field. I'd throw
my backpack over the locked chain-link gate, then
climb up and over. I'd chart a course directly between
Big Daddy's Liquors and the U-Tote-Em, over the
Broward railroad bridge and down the gravel bed, across
the mall parking lot through the front door of Eckerd's
Drugs, out the rear door, across the back parking lot, and
over the crumbling stone wall that was the boundary for
the northwest corner of the golf course.

I explored every square foot of the golf course as if I
owned it. I had read in *National Geographic* that in
northern Brazil there was a tribe of Indians who worked
out the ownership of things according to who loved what
the most. If those beliefs were applied to the golf course
I would have owned the whole thing and I would have
kept it just as it was: wild and undeveloped, a place
where nature was set free.

It must have been a beautifully groomed club in its
prime in the 1930s. It was planted with southern oaks,

drippy with long silver beards of Spanish moss. The yellow pines, positioned to mark the tees, were almost as tall as any building in town. They were wrapped in kudzu and swayed back and forth like giant feather dusters filled with birds. There was a spiral garden of tree ferns leading to a wooden gazebo which had rotted and tilted to one side as though kneeling before the onslaught of unrelenting vegetation. Round beds of white azaleas still bloomed as if they were enormous, puckered golf balls. The sand traps were overgrown with weeds, but the footprint-shaped depressions remained, spread out over the acreage like a dance chart for giants. There were small Spanish-style storage sheds and rain shelters scattered on the grounds. Most had been overrun with bushes and creepers and spiders and everything else that crawled, scratched, twittered, and crunched through the night. The clubhouse was in the most incredible state of decay. It was a two-story stucco building, almost pulpy with a dark green mold. The orange tiled roof had caved in where the joists had been hollowed by termites. The windows were shattered from kids chucking rocks, and the bougainvillea had climbed through the empty frames and scaled the inside walls. The entire structure looked like a past civilization gone belly up. Just the way I liked it.

I felt comfortable there, surrounded by what had been manmade, then abandoned and left to rot. I loved seeing what nature had won back from man. That clash between civilization and vegetation really turned me on. Ruins of ancient cities I had seen in *National Geographic,* such as Machu Picchu, Palenque, and Angkor Wat, which were once great but had fallen and decayed, fascinated me. I stared at those pictures for hours, examining every detail of how the buildings were made, and how they were falling apart. It wasn't only that I was taken with the utterly mysterious way they looked, all crumbling and mossy, but the thrill also came from knowing that a monumental civilization had started, grown, plateaued, peaked, and then crashed and burned. That, at one time, they had had it all and then lost it. The wheels came off and the whole thing just fell apart. And they were finally defeated by something more powerful than all their rules and regulations, elaborate religious beliefs, and best intentions. They were defeated by nature. Not just plants either, but by the inner nature of the people who lived there. The dark side of the soul. The animal instinct. The beast within. Call it what you want, but you just know some bloody, inhuman stuff had to take place for those great cities to collapse. Nature doesn't play favorites. It doesn't know the difference between good and evil. It doesn't negotiate. It just presses forward, always creeping, expanding, unrelenting, always in motion. The vines grow longer, the roots dig deeper, the seeds are cast forward, new vegetation finds nourishment, and soon enough the plants are larger and the cracks lengthen into fissures and the expanding roots divide each stone into fragments as they scale walls and consume entire structures until vast cities disappear beneath a camouflage of leaves.

As far as I'm concerned, vegetation waiting to creep over neglected cities is the same as the wild animal pacing back and forth on the outer edge of the brain. As soon as you stop trying to do your best to do the right thing, or let your guard down for one minute, it comes surging out of the shadows. And just when you think you are better than everyone else, you do something so sinister, so wicked you can't believe you did it. But you did. The moment you think you have it *all*, when you think you are on top, invincible, is probably the last carefree moment you have before you completely screw up and take a fall. And when you reach rock bottom it's every man for himself, and like the people in Machu Picchu, Palenque, and Angkor Wat you'll do anything to survive.

A Child Shall
Lead Them

Here is how it all began. About a month after tenth grade started I was walking to school, and as I did every day, I had followed my desire line. After I climbed over the back gate to the gym playing field and was almost to the rear door of the gym, I noticed a white panel truck drive up onto the field and stop by the gate. I wouldn't have noticed it except for the pair of mounted loud-speakers on top and a sudden crackling burst of sound which ripped across the dry field. I thought the speakers roared "Attention, sinners!" But that seemed so odd to me I figured I'd heard it wrong. I looked around to see if anyone else heard it, but since I was running late there were no other kids on the field. I turned back and watched the truck as it circled around, then slowly am-bled up over the thick crust of asphalt and back onto the road. As the truck passed I noticed the driver. He was a puffy sort of middle-aged man with chunky dark glasses. His hair was so slicked down on his round head that he looked like a polished cockroach. As he passed he glanced at me with wet eyes, intently, as if he were a cop trying to spot a suspect. He slowed down for just a moment, made some sort of decision about me, then gunned the engine. As he did so he grabbed his car phone and started to punch in a number. The truck picked up speed, curved along 69th Street and around the bend. Before I trudged off toward homeroom I glanced back at the field. There was a kid, about sixteen or so, standing out there where the truck had been. He was talking on a cell phone, probably with the guy in the truck, I thought. He was wearing a light-colored striped suit with a white shirt, string tie, and cowboy boots. He planted his legs apart and dug his heels into the packed dirt in front of the locked gate as if he were waiting for someone. I wanted to tell him that the gate was always locked. That it had never been open as far as I knew. And that I was the only person who climbed over it. Everyone else chose to walk out of their way about fifty feet and go around the fence where it stopped at the edge of the road. So I thought that if he was waiting for someone, he had picked the wrong spot.

He finished on the phone and slipped it into his pocket, then raised his hand up over his head and seemed to wave for me to come to him. His other hand held a red book pressed to his chest. Suddenly I had the impression he was a tent-pitching revival preacher, but he was so young. I thought, no way, he's probably some weird new kid whose dad dropped him off at the wrong place. He began to yell in my direction, but the wind was blowing against him and I couldn't make out what he said. Besides, I figured whatever he was screaming about wasn't my problem.

I had problems of my own. I was late for animal duty, which was a kind of detention, only worse. So I turned and trotted toward the science wing. A new shipment of baby pigs, destined for the dissection table, was scheduled to arrive and I knew they'd need feeding and cleaning. When they were hungry they squealed just like infants, gyrated around, and helplessly crapped all over themselves. Charming work. It was a great way to start my day.

I had gotten into trouble two weeks before, after I took a biology exam. When I got my test back from the teacher, Mr. Harvey, I was expecting my usual well-balanced, comfortable C. When it came to grades I wasn't looking to be a "most likely to succeed" type. I didn't want to be class president, or class clown. I just wanted to lie back in my comfort zone and observe the world, like an anthropologist, which was my profession of choice.

But I received an A, just what I didn't want. What were the odds? A million to one? A billion to one? That I would cheat off the girl's test on either side of me, and I would by chance choose only the answers they got correct, and avoid the ones they missed?

And to make it worse, Mr. Harvey knew I was a straight-C student. I had had him for Earth Science the year before and he never once had to write an A on one of my papers. Now he stood in front of the class, held up my test, and said sarcastically, "Well, Walker. This is so much better than your usual mediocre performance. Better than Karen or Wendy's Bs. Better than anyone in the entire class. Than the entire school. Now, I wonder how you managed to do so well?"

Everyone turned in their seats and stared at me. Watched me squirm. Had a laugh at my expense. We all knew what Mr. Harvey was getting at.

The girl on my right, Wendy, had raised an eyebrow when she saw my grade, obviously annoyed that a daydreaming C student could do better than a butt-busting dedicated A student like herself. The girl on my left, Karen Spencer, glared at me and said, acidly, "I hate losers like you." I was shocked, because she had never spoken to me before, maybe never even looked at me before. I was so ashamed I just stared down at the desk and kept my mouth shut. She was a straightforward, mind-your-own-business type, who I figured wouldn't even flinch if I had plopped down a jellied human brain on the lab table.

When I got my test back, I saw that Mr. Harvey had written across the top margin of the page "See me after class." I knew what that was all about.

After class, Mr. Harvey shattered my quiet little comfort zone. He sat down on Karen's lab stool, looked me directly in the eyes, and got right to the point. "You scanned both your neighbors' tests, chose the best answers, and cheated. Didn't you?"

I wanted to say no, but couldn't. Whenever I lied, I got that rock-stuck-in-my-throat feeling. My civics and government teacher talked about people who were so twisted up, so turned around inside, they didn't know when they were lying. They didn't get that rock-stuck-in-their-throat feeling. They couldn't feel the difference between the truth and a lie. Sociopaths are what those people are called, or just plain screwed up. It's supposed to take a lot of years as a liar to get to the point where you don't know the difference. I had, unfortunately, not mastered the art of lying. But I was good at being quiet. So I just sat there and took a few anthropological notes on Mr. Harvey.

He had a pleasant face, olive, with heavy features. Green eyes. Black hair. The longer he paused, the longer became my list of observations. He wore a gold chain. His chest hairs poked through the links; he wore a leather-smelling cologne.

"Why don't you just tell me the truth," he said. "Tell the truth and we'll work this out between us. I won't go to the dean." He held his hands forward, palms up. The no-tricks gesture even monkeys use.

I also had another kind of desire line. Honesty. If I walked in straight lines, I figured, I should talk in straight lines. So I sucked up my gut and told him I cheated. "I was only trying to get a C," I explained. "Can I trade down and call it even?"

He didn't go for the joke. Instead, he gave me animal duty. I'd been at it for two weeks, and still had two weeks to go. It made me feel like the loser Karen had called me, but it was better than being sent to the dean.

After I had turned my back on the kid out in the field I went through a metal door at the back of the science building, took a deep breath of fresh air, and opened the lab door. The rush of formaldehyde was joined with the rank odor of animal waste and discarded rotting parts. I quickly removed a white surgical mask from a box, sprayed it with a can of pine scent, and slipped it over my nose and mouth, then took another breath. Now it just smelled like I was standing on a heap of crap in the middle of a pine forest. From another box I removed a pair of rubber gloves.

Our school prepared their own animal specimens for biology dissections and for other schools in the district. This was done to save money. There were animal pens for baby pigs, birds, and rodents. There was a tadpole and frog pool. Behind that room was another where the animals were prepared by the real sick kids who had

done a lot more than cheat on a test. I always tried to
avoid those kids. I figured if they ran out of animals to
pickle, they'd turn on me.

The baby pigs had arrived and were miserable. They
were in their cages and squealing like enraged infants.
Their eyes were still closed and they were crawling all
over each other, crap squirting every which way while
they tried to find food. "Okay," I hollered. "Daddy's
home!"

They squealed even louder.

I mixed up two gallons of baby formula and filled a
case of clean bottles, then fit them into wire clips so the
pigs could feed from the nipples. That calmed them
enough so I could reach in and sponge down their slimy
pink hides.

The mice I had fed yesterday were already prepared
and in the freezer. But I still had to clean the cages. I
ripped a heavy-duty trash bag off a roll and began to
empty the trays under each row of cages. Then I took the
trays into an open washroom and hosed them down.

Afterward, I fed the worms, tadpoles, and frogs.

When I returned to the pigs they were blissful. I
watched them feed, all lined up in a row as if tucked
under their mother's belly, and I thought of the Peaceable Kingdom painting, where all the animals lived side
by side, and where the lion lies down with the lamb. But
by tomorrow the pigs would be floating in jars of

formaldehyde, having been snuffed out and chopped up by kids who were sentenced to the job, kind of like a chain gang of laughing butchers.

On impulse I grabbed two pigs and two bottles of formula and stuffed them down into my backpack. I zipped it up, slipped it over my shoulders, and headed out the back door. They began to squeal and wrestle around. "Relax," I whispered. "You'll soon be living in paradise." I went straight for the golf-course desire line. No math, civics, history, gym, or English. I aimed myself directly at the duck pond. It was time to lay up in the Peaceable Kingdom, home-school myself with a good book, and listen to the ducks do happy duck things.

"It's a Walker-pig-liberating-holiday," I said to no one in particular as I cruised down the outdoor passageway and headed directly for the gate. But there was someone in my way.

The kid who had been dropped off earlier was standing right in my path. He watched me coming across the field, his face pointy and intent. He was jumpy. I could tell he was excited to see another human. I was probably the first person who had come his way all morning, as there was no gym during the first period. He shifted his weight from foot to foot, smoothed back his shiny black hair, slapped the dust off his jacket with a handkerchief, and wiped the sweat from his face. The closer I got to him, the wider his smile became, until I was standing directly in front of him. He was leering and licking his lips. I felt more like a meal than a person.

I was going to ask him to move out of my path but he beat me to the punch. He lunged forward and shouted into my face, "Do you believe in God?" He thrust the red book at me as if it were a stop sign.

It was a Bible. I didn't answer fast enough.

"Well, do you believe in God?" he wanted to know, and quickly shifted his weight from foot to foot. "Because a lot of people around here don't seem to believe in Him and I want to know about you. I want to put you on the good list." As I stared at him, I could see his eyes were the color of dried blood. That bothered me and he didn't seem so funny anymore.

"Yes," I replied. "I'm Catholic."

He smirked. "Well," he said sharply. "We practice tolerance. But I can baptize you a New Hope Christian right here and now." He kicked at the dirt with his pointy boot to mark the spot, squatted, and set the Bible on the ground. He fished a small amber bottle out of his suit jacket. It looked like a half pint of whiskey. "I got God's cleansing spirit in this water here," he said, giving it a good shake, as though he were going to wake God up and put Him to work.

"No thanks," I replied. I felt myself walking around him, in the same way I walked around bad neighborhood dogs. His eyes followed. I didn't make any sudden moves. He had a dimple in the middle of his chin, which he jutted out, and lined me up with it as though it were a gun sight.

"Then take a pamphlet," he insisted, and whipped one out from inside his jacket and, with the flick of his wrist, snapped it open. There was a picture of a man riding a roller coaster down through the flaming gates of hell. "Here's what awaits sinners, nonbelievers, heretics, and Philistines," he said. "But you can save yourself if you just put your soul in God's hands."

I snatched it out of his hand and pushed it down into my shirt pocket. Suddenly the pigs began to squeal and wiggle around and it occurred to me that I was skipping school and needed to get out of sight. The longer I was waylaid by this preacher kid, the more likely I'd be busted. I looped my backpack over the top of the gate and began to hook my fingers and shoes into the chain-link diamonds.

"Hey," he hollered, and pointed the Bible at me. "My mission is to clean this place up. I know some filthy *business* goes on in there." He pointed a corner of the Bible toward the school. "You wanna join me?"

"Thanks. But no thanks," I replied and scrambled to the top, regained my balance, and hopped down.

"Well, I'm lookin' for sinners," he said bluntly. "I got the cure for 'em. If you see any, send 'em out here." He shook the little bottle and grinned at me.

"Try reading the personals," I replied.

"Hey!" he shouted. He spoke so loudly his head jerked back as if he'd been punched. "Remember, Jesus said the wages of sin is death and the wicked shall be turned into hell."

"I've read the Bible," I said. "I know what it says."

"Then why don't you tell some of your friends to come out here and visit with me. Tell 'em to come tomorrow. My dad and the rest of us are puttin' in a church across the street, and I'll bring a special treat."

"I don't have any friends," I said, and immediately regretted letting him know anything about me.

"You got a friend in Jesus," he quickly replied, and then he winked at me. "Amen."

His wink was like some kind of confidential signal. Some kind of wet-finger-wiggling secret-club hand-shake. It sent a shiver across my shoulders. It was as if he counted me among his friends, whether I agreed to be one or not. I had a sudden feeling that he was insane. I simply thought, he's a nut. Not the kind of nuts you see who drift about talking gibberish and picking their noses in public. Or the wrist-slashing type they fish out of bloody bathtubs. But the Hitler type.

I unhooked my backpack and the pigs began to squeal.

"What you got in there?" he asked.

"None of your business," I snapped back.

"Animal sacrifice?" he guessed, eager to accuse me of something wicked.

I didn't say anything back to him. I knew he was going to have the last word whether I let him or not, so I just turned and took off.

It had rained the night before but the ground had dried under the morning sun and cracked into pieces. It looked like a field of broken pottery shards. As I hustled down my path I thought, someone should do something about the preacher kid. There were laws against people selling anything on school property, and I guessed there were laws against people preaching and digging for dirt. But it wasn't going to be me. That was outside my comfort zone.

A Secret in Mothballs

After I left the preacher boy I passed over the railroad bridge, through the mothball-smelling aisles of Eckerd's Drugs, entered the northwest corner of the golf course, and took a deep breath. I wanted some fresh air. I loved being out among the trees and sunlight and away from that puzzle of hallways, tiny airless rooms, and fluorescent lights. School was claustrophobic. Plus, it always smelled faintly of the formaldehyde and animal waste of the lab. Because the building was air-conditioned, all the air from the animal pens was recirculated. And even though it passed through a filter, the smell of brine and pickled specimens and animal crap never quite went away. That's why, when I followed my path from school to the golf course, I always walked through Eckerd's. They had the strongest, most intense mothball-smelling air in the world. The first time I went in there I thought I was going to puke or pass out. I had to turn around and leave. I stood bent over in the parking lot, clutching a handicap-parking sign for support, gagging, until I caught my breath. What kind of store, I asked myself, would be stupid enough to make their air smell so foul that you couldn't breath it long enough to make a purchase? Then I thought, maybe it wasn't the store, maybe it was all the old people haunting the aisles, all jammed up in the pain-reliever section, wearing sweaters they kept in mothball-bombed closets. But it was the store. It was as if old people had a pathological fear of Florida moths and Eckerd's had figured out if they filtered their air through mothballs, old folks would just pack the place and stay there and buy stuff all day long. It seemed to have worked. The store was always filled with the cardigan crowd.

I never bought too much stuff there. Even the breath mints tasted of mothballs. I generally cruised up and down the aisles, taking a few deep cleansing breaths, waving my arms up over my head, until I felt my lungs and clothes had been purified of animal smell, and people fifty feet away couldn't tell that I went to Jefferson High. By the time I'd made it out the back door I reeked of mothballs. When I entered the golf course I cried out, "I am the anti-Mothra." I waved my arms overhead. A cloud of adult moths and their children rose up over the treetops, screeching, fleeing. Even Mothra would run if she got one whiff of me.

The mothball smell didn't clear my head, though. I couldn't stop thinking about the preacher boy. He must have heard what had happened at our school last year and was now sniffing around to see if there was any left-over dirt to dig up. There had been a big stink because a French teacher, Mr. LaBlanc, had come out of the closet. I didn't think anyone would care how Mr. LaBlanc ran his private life. But I was way off in my thinking. As it turned out, the entire town cared about Mr. LaBlanc's private life. It was a headline in the local newspaper the evening he outed himself. GAY TEACHER REQUESTS SPOUSAL BENEFITS. The article went on to say that Mr. LaBlanc had requested his long-time companion, Mr. Klein, be covered by the health benefits he received as a teacher in Broward County. The county was refusing to extend benefits to what it defined as "lifestyle choices based on alternative morality." Whatever that meant.

A Christian Parents League suddenly appeared out of nowhere and picketed the school, protesting against "homosexual recruitment" while handing out leaflets which quoted Old Testament scripture against "Sodomite Teachers." Other protesting parents just quoted what slurs they had learned over a lifetime of reading bathroom walls. And the students were just as mean, hunting him down like dogs, all around the school and throughout the town. He couldn't step out of his house without someone yelling something nasty in his face. At school the students referred to him as "Kermit the faggot," and the administration, which was trying to be neutral, finally caved in. They gave him the golden boot in the ass. They paid him an undisclosed amount of money and Mr. LaBlanc took his French books elsewhere. Since then there'd been no sign of the Christian Parents League or the like at school, until the preacher dad and his preaching son lined us up in their self-righteous sights.

I don't know exactly when Fort Lauderdale became a mecca for storefront preachers. They must have had a Bible convention out in the sticks and decided there were a lot of rich sinners here who wanted to pay off their guilt. They came out of the Everglades and central Florida cow towns like an Old Testament plague, rented cheap space in crummy strip malls between beauty schools and karate clubs, put out signs announcing their special brand of salvation, then marched boldly around town passing out leaflets which basically told everyone they were going to burn in hell for not being true believers. They were always going on about devil worship, adultery, sexual perversion, abortion, school prayer, government conspiracies, and more. They were way too weird, and too scruffy, and were always asking for money. Even the normal born-again religious types avoided them.

The easy converts must have been drying up. So they were out on witch-hunts, chasing after abortion doctors, picketing movie theaters that showed anything with a PG rating, chaining themselves to the courthouse to protest for school-prayer reform. So I figured the preacher boy was just out on our gym field fishing for dirt like the rest of them, and trying to collect Brownie points from God.

The truth was that I *had* a secret, and I didn't want this little Bible-thumping rodent sniffing it out. The secret concerned Karen Spencer, the girl whose test I'd cheated off of. I knew she was a lesbian, and I had seen her screwing around with Jennifer Owet, another girl in our sophomore class. I had discovered them that summer, at the duck pond. But what I knew I kept a secret, because I only knew this stuff by accident, and it was dangerous information. I'd been at Jefferson High School long enough to know that the place was definitely *not* what could be called a sexually liberated institution. There was plenty of sex, of course, but same-sex sex was still hidden deep in the closet. The few people who were suspected of being gay were treated like walking AIDS transmitters until they somehow arranged a few dates with the opposite sex, or transferred to another school, or just stopped coming altogether. What Karen and Jennifer did was none of my business, and I kept my mouth shut.

Besides, they were mine to study. I observed them at the pond. I watched them at school. I followed them around town. To myself, I called them my "Wild Kingdom" couple. They were my secret, and my private show.

I was pretty certain I was the only one who knew because I only found out by accident.

During the summer I had been camping overnight at the duck pond when they sneaked up on me. I had stretched my camouflage tarp between two small ficus trees on one side of the water. I had my Walkman on and couldn't hear anything but the disc jockey from WRBD announcing another Coltrane number when I saw a beam from a flashlight sweep over the water. Whoever held the light was methodically searching the area. Not close to the ground, as if they had lost their keys, but making sure no one was around to see what they were about to do. The beam of light, the round mirror and centered light bulb, a white hand and wrist was all I could make out. I turned off Coltrane, yanked the headset down around my neck, and froze. My first thought was that someone was going to dump a body. There had been a lot of organized-crime activity reported lately in the paper. The Cuban and Haitian mobs were blowing each other away over crack and meth labs, dope imports, prostitution, and all the usual vice stuff. Bodies had been turning up in odd places, so I thought I was about to witness some gruesome act, like some guy with cement shoes going for a one-way swim.

The hand with the flashlight separated the pond and area into four zones. North, south, east, and west. I was north, they were west. The hand first sprayed the light

back and forth in close strokes across its own zone. Then
slowly it scanned the south and the east. When it moved
into my zone I held my breath and lowered my face into
the wadding of my army-surplus sleeping bag. I closed
my eyes. My mind was racing. If these are big-time crim-
inals, I thought, they'll blow me away too. I could tell the
light was getting closer and closer, because of the hissing. It wasn't the light that made the sound but the startled insects scrabbling through the leaves and twigs.
Then the light must have passed over my head and camouflage tarp, as there were about two seconds of silence
and then it moved off to the northwest, where the insects
continued to scatter. Finally, after the entire area had
been searched, the light returned to the feet of the person. I saw brown hiking boots, and jeans. Then the light
switched off. My heart was pounding, and slowly I began
to breathe.

"It's clear," whispered a girl's voice.

"Good," replied a second girl.

I raised my head. I had an open view across the pond.
The ducks were sleeping with their single legs planted
on the ground and their beaks tucked into their wings.
There was enough moonlight to make out the green
feathers of the males and the white banded necks of the
females. Then I saw a naked leg, a girl's leg, just one. It
hopped up and about as she tugged her jeans down and
stepped out. She moved into a stream of moonlight and

in one motion pulled her T-shirt up over her head. She wasn't wearing a bra. The other girl stepped up behind her and ran her hands around her waist then slowly up her sides, up over her breasts, up her shoulders, up her neck, over her face, and stopped at her eyes. She said something, then laughed.

It was my future lab partner, Karen Spencer, and Jennifer Owet, a girl who played drums in the school band.

Jennifer spun around. As she did so I saw Karen was naked. The moon was low behind her. The outline of her skin was white as chalk around the dark shadow of her body.

What was I feeling at that moment? Seeing them, without them seeing me. Spying on them. Taking my time to look at them. Their breasts, their bellies, even lower, all so beautiful, so sexy. My heart was no longer pounding in fear, but with desire. I wanted to join them, but I was frozen. I couldn't move a muscle. And the only thing I was really certain of is that they had absolutely no desire to see me. And it hit me that I was seeing something very private, something I shouldn't see, nor should anyone else. Still, I couldn't turn my eyes away. It was worse than cheating off of someone's test. It was like peeking into someone's bedroom window. If I stood up and said "Hi, I'm here too," I didn't know what they'd do, but I was sure they wouldn't welcome me with open arms.

So I kept it a secret. It was a gift for me alone, and it

was an unopened gift to them that I didn't say a word to
another person. Not a soul. Not that I knew anyone I
could tell anyway. But telling someone would be the
same as if I found some trigger-happy bird hunters and
brought them back to my pond and said, "Look, fellas,
ducks. Blaze away!" No, the girls had become a part of
the pond now, part of the Peaceable Kingdom painting
where we all got along. Except I saw myself as a deviant
part of the picture. There I was, behind all the innocent
animals and people, hiding under a bush like a pervert,
alone and turned on, watching them while I was too gut-
less to step out into the light.

Jennifer had inched forward and lowered her foot into
the water. "Come on," she said.

Karen lit a match, then a string of candles, and set
them into the limestone shelf.

Jennifer dove into the water and disappeared. When
she surfaced she whipped her wet hair back over her
head and breathed loudly.

Karen jumped in, one arm pressed across her breasts,
the other hand pinching her nose. She popped right up
and sputtered, treading water and pushing her hair from
her eyes. The ducks woke up and quacked, put up a fuss
then settled down again.

Jennifer casually swam around her. They didn't talk
much. They seemed like a couple who had already
talked about themselves, who they were, what they liked,

what other people might think of them. But I wanted to
talk with them. I wanted to ask all the obvious questions.
What's it like kissing? What's it like having sex? What's
it like being the same? What's it like having to hide?
What's it like being so brave? After all my months at the
duck pond I had never gone swimming. Never dared
take off my clothes and dive in. I only looked at the
water, watched the ducks, listened to the wind in the
trees. I fit into the duck pond like a cement statue of St.
Francis in a garden.

Jennifer turned over onto her back and began to float.
Gently she waved her arms and drifted across the pond,
her orange hair fanned out behind her, shining, her lips
open, her milky breasts just above the water. She looked
like Ophelia serenely floating down the stream.

Karen paddled over to the bank and carefully crawled
up and over the jagged stone ledge. She found her bag
and tugged out a white towel. It unrolled, and beneath
the moonlight it glowed. She rough-dried her hair, then
wrapped the towel around her body and tucked the loose
flap under her arm. She stooped down and removed a
cigarette from a pack, turned, and lit it off the candle.
She took a deep drag.

"What are you doing tomorrow?" she asked.

Jennifer exhaled and slipped beneath the water.
When she surfaced she said, "I don't know. Music
lessons. Give me a drag."

Karen leaned forward. But before she gave Jennifer the cigarette she kissed her. It was a long, soft kiss.

A cloud drifted in front of the moon and everything went almost dark again.

"It's late," she said. "I have to get back." She dried her hair and began to dress.

"Where's the flashlight?" Karen asked.

"I put it on the ground next to the clothes," Jennifer replied.

I heard Karen rustling through the leaves. "I can't find it," she said. "Help me. It's Dad's police light and he'll kill me if he finds it missing."

She must have hit it with her foot before she found it with her hands. "Ouch, got it," she said, sounding relieved. She turned it on and tied her shoes.

"Let's go," Jennifer said. They held hands and walked, Karen following Jennifer between the trees.

I stood frozen in the bushes for about an hour before I even dared move.

Then I went back the next night. They didn't show. I went the next. They didn't show. I went every night. They didn't show until exactly one week later. And again, one week after that. I kept going until I figured out they were on a weekly schedule, every Thursday night, like clockwork. And if anyone wanted to know what I did on my Thursday nights, I'd just smile and say, "I never miss an episode of 'Wild Kingdom.'

Anthropology 101

I was still thinking about the girls and the preacher boy when I spotted the remains of the old Ford Falcon that someone dumped in a sand trap ages ago. As I approached I thought maybe I could build a pig cage in the trunk. I could line the bottom with grass and leaves, drive some holes through the trunk lid, and tie it closed. I didn't know what might happen to the pigs if I set them loose. Maybe stray dogs would get them. There were raccoons around, snakes and hawks, and if they wandered beyond the golf course cars would flatten them on the road. If I was going to play God to the animals, setting them up to be road kill was too cruel.

But when I looked inside the car I didn't think it was safe for the pigs. Humans had claimed the car for their own playpen. Across the ripped-open and charred upholstery were the fresh remains of a party: beer cans, grocery-store bags, fast-food wrappers, and cigarette butts. A typical golf-course bash. I set my backpack on the ground and stuck my head through the side window. I imagined what went on the night before. It wasn't difficult to re-create the action. Someone said, "Hey, let's have a party at the golf course." Then someone else said, "Hey, let's get some beer." And someone else said, "Hey, I have a fake ID."

Before I touched anything I studied it all very carefully, memorized it better than any test material. I kept my anthropologist's objective point of view. I was someone who was studying the evidence of a curious people and culture. Anthropologists don't search through ancient garbage and complain about litterbugs. They love the garbage. They celebrate when they find garbage left over from another time. They learn from it. Study it. Sift through it. Hardly touch it, not wanting to spoil it. They just want to understand it. They map it out, label it, record it, and move on, searching for more garbage.

I had my hand shoved down into the crack of the back seat as if I were searching for loose change when I found a square foil package with an advertisement printed on the side. DON'T GET LOST IN THE DARK. NEW NEON PARTY COLORS. RED, GREEN, BLUE, YELLOW. The condom packet was still a bit sticky with lubricant, so I knew it had belonged to last night's party.

And voilà! There was the condom, stuffed into the ashtray mounted in the elbow rest on the inner door. I got a stick and fished the used neon-green condom out of the rusty cup. It was a color I had not seen before in other golf-course love nests. And I guessed that after someone had said, "I have a fake ID," someone else said, "Hey, how about some safe sex?"

I had also spotted an unsmoked cigarette on the back dashboard of the Falcon. It reminded me of Jennifer and Karen, smoking in the dark, kissing, exhaling pillows of smoke filled with the moonlight.

I was reaching in to pick up the cigarette when I heard the first explosion. It wasn't a car backfire or a shotgun. It was something that went off like a stick of dynamite. Overhead, a frantic cluster of quacking ducks circled, scrambled into formation, then peeled off. I was looking up at them when there was a second blast. Above me, something splattered, blew apart, as if someone were shooting skeet. But it wasn't skeet. I hunched down behind the fender as a mangled land turtle hit the ground next to me. A smoking, shredded strip of duct tape was ripped open over what had been the belly. All that was left was a pulpy cavity. All four legs were missing, but the head was still attached by a strand of white tendon. The shell was split open like a coconut and blood oozed out, shiny and thick.

Then before I could get to my feet Mal Guss ran out from the tree line and tackled me. He flipped me over, jammed his knees into my shoulders, and pinned my wrists above my head. I cocked my head back and looked up at him. "Get off 'a me," I said. "Get off!"

"Make me," he replied, and juked his knee a little

deeper into my back. "Come on, nature boy, make your move."

"Get off!" I hollered.

I knew him, his twin brother, and their friends from bumping into them during animal duty. Mr. Harvey put him to work on the killing side of the lab. He was one of nature's predators.

A couple of centuries ago, when wealthy nobility designed acres of elaborate, perfectly planted gardens, they felt something was missing. It was all too safe. The Peaceable Kingdom was too tame. So they hired real lunatics to live in specially built grottoes and hollow trees and caves. Then they'd let their guests roam the gardens and every so often they'd turn a corner and a yowling maniac would jump out and give them a good scare and chase them up and down the paths, just to let them know that nature wasn't all toothless animal topiaries and wood nymphs. That it was still full of dark surprises. I'd love to have been there. It must have been a wild scene, all those genteel men and women with tall powdered wigs and yellow satin outfits and high-heeled shoes prancing down the mossy paths followed by some hunched-over toothless nut dressed in burlap and waving a tree root overhead.

With Mal's knees digging into my shoulders, it didn't feel like some playacting lunatic had tackled me. It felt like I was being mugged. Then he spotted the turtle and hopped off.

I sprang to my feet.

"Awesome," he shouted and picked it up. "Hey, Mike," he called to his twin brother, "come see this."

Mike, and another friend of theirs, Stephanelli, crashed through the branches of low trees and trotted over to where we were standing.

Stephanelli pulled his bangs open across his eyes. They were more like curtains, really. His head was the same bullet shape you find in collections of medieval armor. He was skinny with bad skin and freckles. I always had the impression he was so reckless he would do anything.

"Pinhead," Mal ordered, "give me another M-80 and the tape."

Stephanelli tugged them out of his backpack.

"Hey, Walker," Mike asked, as Mal set another charge. "What are you doing here?"

"Minding my own business," I replied.

"You sure you're not minding something else?" He pointed to the condom, which was still draped over the back fender where I'd left it.

"That's not mine," I said.

Stephanelli laughed through his nose. Since I couldn't see his eyes I looked at his teeth. He was all Stonehenge.

Mal had the turtle in one hand, and the lighter in the other. "I'm going to count to five," he said, and nodded toward me. "And then I'm gonna heave this turtle grenade up your butt."

"One," Stephanelli counted. "Two."

"I'm not screwing around here, Walker. You better put it in gear," Mal said, warning me.

I should have made a stand right there. I should have said, No, I'm not going to run. And if Mal had said something like, Hey, it's fight or flight, I should have sucker-punched him square in the face. But I didn't punch him or even attempt to make a stand. And once you cave in, you can't go back to making a stand. Being a coward is one reputation you can never get over. You might as well pack up all your stuff, move to a new neighborhood, get plastic surgery, and start all over again like someone in a Witness Protection Program.

"Better get your butt in motion," slobbered Stephanelli. He held up three fingers.

I grabbed my backpack from the ground and took off through the trees. I got about ten steps in when the explosion went off overhead. I heard branches crack. I heard the three of them braying, and I just kept running. When I knew I was out of turtle-throwing distance, I slowed down to listen.

"Walker," Mike hollered. "Come on back. We were just fooling around."

Even from where I was, I could hear Stephanelli's nose-honking laugh.

"Walker," Mike repeated. "We got a deal to make with you. Come on back. We're starting a club."

"Yeah," Stephanelli hollered. "We need your help moving the clubhouse."

"Fire in the hole!" Mal shouted.

The explosion was about twenty feet to my right. They must have taped rocks around the M-80, because it felt as though I was being peppered with buckshot. My ears were still ringing when the second one blew up in the tree behind me.

"Charge!" yelled Stephanelli. I heard him crashing through the bushes. Then an explosion went off and he hollered. "Cut that crap out! That thing bounced off my head before it went off."

"Then it hit you in the one place besides your ass that's useless," Mal yelled.

There was another fuse hiss and explosion.

"Aw, crap!" Stephanelli yowled, and thrashed around. "That really sucked. Aw, crap."

"What is with you, man?" Mike said to Mal. "You blew up our idiot."

I could hear Mal tromp through the undergrowth. "Quit your whinin' and stand still," he said, disgusted. "It's hardly bleedin'."

"It burns," he whimpered. "Don't touch it."

"I hope you never have to fight a war," Mal replied. "You wouldn't last as long as it takes me to piss."

"What?" Stephanelli asked. "What? I can't hear a thing. I think you popped my eardrum."

"Put a cork in it!" Mal hollered. "Did you hear that?"

I stood there, motionless, not wanting to be their next casualty. After seeing what they had done to the turtle, I didn't want them to know I had the pigs, which must have had some survival instinct kick in, because with Mike and Mal around they didn't make a sound.

Stephanelli was moaning as if he had a mortal head wound, and Mal was giving him grief. I figured they had disregarded me, so I turned and quietly slipped between the trees. I had one exit in mind, "the path of least resistance," and it took me away from them.

The Snake

The next morning, after I fed the pigs out in the back yard, I followed my desire line to school. It led me directly to Mike, Mal, and Stephanelli, whose damaged right ear was shielded beneath a plastic Tupperware bowl. The bowl was fastened to his head with masking tape. He reached up and gently adjusted it as though it were part of an elaborate hairdo. That was the first thing I saw, until I noticed the moccasin.

The preacher boy held it in his hands. It was sandy-colored, with brown links running up its back. It was only about three feet long. I didn't know if it was mature enough to be deadly, but I wasn't going to experiment either. I had seen snake-handling preachers on TV, and there was a lot of snake handling at Seminole Indian mission churches out in the Everglades. Down by the preacher boy's foot was a small wooden crate with a wire-mesh gate. NEW HOPE HOUSE OF GOD was stenciled along one side in red letters. HANDLE WITH CARE, on the other. Standing next to him was a kid who had to be his younger brother. Another preacher boy. They were dressed alike in the same striped cotton suit, white shirt, string tie, and cowboy boots that were as spit-polished as their black hair was shiny with pomade. There must have been about twenty kids standing around, watching the boys, then glancing over their shoulders to see if any teachers were coming to break it up. But none were on the back side of the school. They were out front pulling bus duty, or smoking a last butt in the teacher's lavatory.

Just then there was a buzz from the preacher boy's pocket. "Excuse me," he said, and dug his cell phone out. He turned away from us and listened.

Over his shoulder I spotted the white van with the loudspeaker on top. It was parked off the road a couple hundred yards down the street. I wondered if it was the man in the van calling. Maybe it was his father, the preaching dad.

The preacher boy nodded a few times, then said something into the phone and hung up. When he turned back to face us he seemed nervous. "I've been advised not to handle the snake on school property," he announced. "But we can walk over to the field just across the road." He pointed in that direction. "We own that property. We're gonna put a church on it." Already there was a small hand-painted sign staked into the sand which announced the imminent arrival of the NEW HOPE HOUSE OF GOD.

"Then let's do it," Mal said. "I got to see this action."

The preacher boy led the way like a Pied Piper, with us following him, and the younger brother with the large boom box pulling up the rear.

Once we regrouped the older preacher boy held the snake out at arm's length. The brother turned on the boom box and began to sing along with a hymn. The preacher boy swayed back and forth and drifted around to the music, waiting to find an entrance as though stepping into a line dance. He closed his eyes, raised his one hand up over his head, and slipped into a rapturous two-step. The younger brother sang "Marching to Jesus, marching to Jesus . . . We'll come a' marching to Jesus when he calls . . ."

The snake took all that swinging about in stride. Its tail curled up and hooked around, not unlike a cat's tail, and its tongue slithered in and out, and its eyes blinked. Actually, it looked sluggish.

I thought this was one of the oddest things I had ever seen and it threw me right into my anthropologist zone. I wished I had a video camera to record it all, not just the snake and evangelists but the kids watching, too. They stood there, almost hypnotized, with a big round "Wow" stuck between their lips. And I felt the same way. It wasn't every day someone came to school and waltzed around with a poisonous snake.

Suddenly Mal stepped forward and reached for the moccasin. "Give me that," he commanded. "I'll show you how to dance with a killer."

The preacher boy's eyes flipped open as if he were a ventriloquist's dummy come to life. We all took a step back as he swung the snake away from Mal and held it up over his head. "I'm not allowed to let anyone touch this snake," he said gravely. "It could bite. It could kill you."

"My ass," Mal snapped back. "That snake's half asleep. Now hand it over or I'll take it from you. Your choice." Then he turned to the brother who was still singing. "Cut the noise."

The boy froze for a moment, then looked toward his older brother for orders.

Stephanelli began to bray like a donkey, and with the way his ear was covered, everyone began to laugh. I looked closely at the preacher boy. I could see the annoyance cross his face. He had lost control of his open-field congregation. But he fought back.

"Turn it off," the preacher boy said to his brother. "Besides, we don't want this snake to get excited when I give it to this"—he sized Mal up—"Man of God."

He turned and held the snake out at arm's length. "Be careful," he warned. "It can bite you, and we don't believe in snakebite kits where I come from."

Mal gripped the snake around its middle and the

preacher slowly released his hand. "What's his name?" Mal asked.

"Judas," said the younger brother, on cue, the word jumping out of his mouth like a spark.

"Well, Mr. Judas," Mal said, holding the snake above his head and staring up into its eyes. "When did you last eat?"

"This morning," the preacher replied.

"Well, hell," Mal shot back. "No wonder he won't bite. He won't bite me even if I bit him first. He's not hungry enough."

"He's plenty hungry," the preacher replied. "It's just the devil hasn't entered him yet today."

"Well, let me see you dance him around when he hasn't eaten for a few weeks." He tossed the snake straight up toward the preacher, as though it were a baseball bat and they were planning to pick sides.

The preacher grabbed the snake around the neck and swiftly pressed his thumb down on its triangular skull. He grinned and gave a quick nod. The snake's tongue slipped out like a split flame and tasted the air.

"You win," Mal said, pointing to the preacher's thumb. "So you get to pick first."

The preacher looked confused, as if he was from another country. He didn't follow the baseball lead, and he didn't seem to know what to expect from Mal. He glanced at his younger brother. His little lap-dog face was all pinched together, as though he was ready to snap at the first one who dared get close to him. It made me think they had been in this situation before, and right at this juncture things didn't turn out so well for them.

"Hey," the preacher boy shouted, and hunkered down with his eyes flashing. He seemed to have found some renewed strength. He held the head of the snake straight out at Mal, aiming the thin-lipped snout at him as if it were a handgun. "I think you're just the man to help me!"

"With what?" Mal asked.

The preacher boy pointed the snake at me and shook his head in disgust. "I'm lookin' for ho-mo-sexuals," he drawled in a matter-of-fact way, finally saying what I knew he meant all along. "I've talked to this guy, and he's no help. He acts like he's got something to hide." He turned back toward Mal. "But I bet a guy like you knows what Jesus meant when He said, 'The wicked shall be turned into hell.' "

"I do," Mal said and smiled as if he were proud to be one of the wicked. "I know exactly what that means."

"So tell me," the preacher boy said, stepping closer to Mal. "What do you know about ho-mo-sexuals at this school that I should know?"

"I know that if you dial 1-900-BIG-BOYS on your lit-tle cell phone, you'll get all the ho-mo sin-'n-skin you can handle."

Stephanelli was right on cue, laughing through his nose and braying. His Tupperware shield had slipped up over his ear and onto the top of his head as if it were a pillbox hat. His exposed ear, shiny with burn salve, was blistered and raw where the skin was seared from the blast. The rest of the students joined right in with Stephanelli.

"That's not funny," the preacher boy said stiffly. Then he looked out at all of us who were still laughing. "I'm not lookin' for humor. I'm lookin' for ho-mo-sexuals, for those who are destined to burn in a lake of everlasting fire. And I'm going to find 'em. Mark my words."

Before any more was said the morning bell sounded for homeroom and we all began to drift back across the road. Most everyone went toward the rear door of the auditorium for a football pep rally. I headed for the science wing and animal duty. If the exchange between Mal and the preacher boy had signaled the first round of the fight, Mal was ahead on a knockdown.

But as the preacher boy lowered his snake into its cage he suddenly had something more to say. "I'll be here all day," he shouted across the field with one hand cupped around his mouth. "We'll be putting the church together soon. If any of you know something, come tell me. Slip me a note. It'll be our secret. You all hear me?"

How could we not have heard him? He was like an Old Testament teenager wailing from the mountaintop.

It Felt So Good

I called the auditorium the Sports Memorial Hate Center because football, basketball, and every other sports pep rally was held there. Any time I could avoid attending a rally, I did.

Our mascot was an old Confederate general dressed in a gray uniform and waving the Stars and Bars. Of course, as was explained so many times by the school superintendent, the faithful general and the Confederate flag did not stand for slavery and racism, but "For the cultural history of the Old South." Never mind if you asked any true Southerner they would tell you that Florida was *not* the South, was *not* a true part of the Confederacy. Sure, they belonged to the Confederacy, but they didn't really do much for the war effort. Not like Georgia or the Carolinas or Virginia. So really, our school borrowed a mascot from another place. And if you figured the town of Jefferson had absolutely no Confederate history of its own, not a plantation, not one row of cotton, not even a regiment that skirmished with Union soldiers, then they had no legitimate reason to choose the mascot they did. We could have been the Gators, or the Bull-dogs, or the Wild Horses, anything. But no. With a world of choices before them, our school chose a Confederate general, a staunch defender of the right to own slaves. That was not an accident. And it was no accident that I skipped every rally.

When I had finished feeding the pigs and mice I went into the reptile room and stood over the frog tank. "Today you are liberated," I shouted. "Pack your little green bags. It's back-to-nature time." I put a dozen of them into a paper sack and hid them in my backpack.

As I walked across the gym field I could hear the school band playing "Dixie" so I knew the pep rally was winding down. I picked up speed, but once again the preacher boy was straddling my path in front of the gate.

"I thought you were going to build a church today," I said, pulling up in front of him.

He shrugged. "It's supposed to come on a truck. But it hasn't arrived yet," he replied, and changed the subject. "How'd you like the snake?"

"Don't even ask," I replied. "You know I think you're a head case."

"But you're a Christian," he said. "We got that in common."

"Look," I said. "We have nothing in common."

"Well, I'll tell you a secret and then we'll have something in common."

I didn't want to hear about his secrets, but before I could get around him he spoke.

"I think there's something wrong with you that nobody knows but you and me and God," he whispered, and clapped the dirt from his hands. "I was wondering how you feel about the opposite sex?"

"You're an asshole," I said. "Now out of my way."

"Tell me the truth," he asked, and leaned toward me. "Tell me and I won't say another word."

"I like women," I said, exasperated, and stepped around him. But before I could take two steps he broke his promise.

"That's nice," he said smoothly. "Very nice. But honestly, that's not what I'm troubled with. I'm more concerned with how you feel about men."

I was so angry each word came out of my mouth like a knife blade stabbing at him. "Well," I said. "This is what you should be troubled with. If you don't stop messing with me I'm going to knock the crap out of you." Then I walked on, threw my backpack over the fence, and began to scramble up the side.

"Hey," he shouted, looking at me from over his shoulder, "God is going to clean up this school. And I'm going to be the one standing on the mountain looking down at the fallen. I know where I'll be. But you better figure where you'll be. There ain't no room to sit on the fence in God's kingdom."

I shot him the finger, then jumped down onto my side.

He ran forward and pressed himself against the fence. "I'll make a deal with you," he said in a conspiratorial whisper. "Just tell me who the deviants are at this school. I just want to talk with them, make 'em see the light. If you help me, then I'll leave you alone."

"Don't push me," I snarled and kept going.

The frogs were croaking so much and thumping around inside my backpack that I bypassed Eckerd's and went directly to the pond. I opened the bag and shook them out.

"You've been liberated," I announced with great fanfare. "You are free to roam the Peaceable Kingdom."

Almost instantly, a duck waddled over and in one swallow ate an entire baby frog. Another frog leaped into the water and began to swim. A fish I had never seen before came up from below, its large mouth unhinged, and it scooped the frog into its belly, rolled over, and disappeared. The rest of the frogs scattered into the underbrush, fleeing for their lives. The Peaceable Kingdom theory did not take into account the food chain or the survival of the fittest.

That thought deflated me, and I was hopping around like a frog myself, trying to recapture them, when I

spotted Karen and Jennifer cutting across the fairway
and heading in my direction. They must also have
skipped the rally.

I swore, and turned and ran bent over toward the
other side of the pond. I worked my way deep enough
into a stand of low scrub palms and lay down. From my
vantage point, through the overlapping fronds, I could
just barely see them. I was sure they couldn't see me.

I waited in the bushes for them to do something sexy.
But they didn't. It wasn't one of their "Wild Kingdom"
Thursday nights. They just sat on the ground, back to
back, like bookends without books between them. They
were smoking cigarettes and talking, but with the wind
blowing through the leaves everything they said sounded
like radio static. I wished I could hear them. I had seen
them naked, but I had never really had a chance to over-
hear an entire conversation. I mean, they might talk
about things that are totally secret to dykes, subjects I
knew nothing about. Of course, they might not talk about
anything interesting at all. Mrs. German had told us
about some literary types who once arranged to have
James Joyce meet with Marcel Proust. Everyone was
excited to have these two genius literary minds of the
twentieth century meet and converse. People sat in a circle of chairs around the great men and waited to hear
what the combination of these two minds would produce.
So after Joyce and Proust took their seats they just sat

and complained about their physical ailments. Joyce said his eyes were failing. Proust said that loud noises gave him headaches. They both had liver problems. All they did was swap aches and pains like any two old farts in a nursing home. There was nothing brilliant about their conversation. As it turned out, the geniuses were pretty normal, and not freaks of nature. Everyone was disappointed.

That's how Karen and Jennifer seemed to me. Normal. Calm, like any two people. Then it hit me. They're calm, I thought, because they don't yet know about the preacher boy and his mission. Because if I was gay and someone was hanging around school looking to drag me out of the closet, saying all gays were perverted freaks who were going to burn in hell, I'd be pretty pissed off. I would not be calm, smoking a cigarette and letting the day unfold without a fight.

This wasn't the first time I thought it was up to me to say something to them. To warn them. Once, I was following them down Las Olas Boulevard, which was way over on the east side of town. By coincidence we had gone to the same movie. *Lady Chatterley's Lover* was playing at an old downtown theater that showed classic films. Mrs. German had assigned all her English classes to read something by D. H. Lawrence, and, like me, the girls must have thought the movie was a lot easier to handle. After the show they started walking up the

street, window shopping. Maybe because I had just seen
the movie I was still in the mood to watch things. So I
followed them at a distance. They didn't do anything any
other girls wouldn't do, except they were holding hands,
and bumping shoulders and hips, and getting real close
to kissing each other when they talked. Because I knew
their secret, I knew every gesture meant more than just
chummy girl friendship. But I could tell they were nervous about it. When some kid let out a yell, or a car
passed by too loudly, or a person suddenly dashed out of
a store in front of them, their hands uncoupled like train
cars yanked apart. But after a few moments their hands
always found each other again.

I had watched them for about ten minutes when I saw
a cop car coming up the street. I was lurking in front of
the World of Leather, not doing anything wrong, and just
checking out the leather accessories, which looked a lot
like medieval torture-chamber wear. But I knew Karen's
dad was a cop, and I thought if he was in that car, he
probably wouldn't like what the girls were doing. I just
stopped and watched the car cruise up the street like a
silent torpedo. My first impulse was to yell something
out, anything, that would make them pull apart. But I
didn't. I just stood there and watched as the squad car
came into their view. As soon as Karen saw it she jerked
her hand back and took a hard left into a Radio Shack.
Jennifer just stood out in the street looking down at her

feet, rubbing her fingers, which had just about been
snapped off, until Karen poked her head out. I didn't
hear what Jennifer said, but she must have given her the
all-clear, or told her not to be so paranoid or something,
because they continued up the street. But not holding
hands.

Now, I thought. Just step out of the bushes and say
hello. You have the perfect excuse. You have some stale
bread in your backpack and you can say you stopped by
to feed the ducks. You can apologize for cheating off of
Karen's test. You can drift into a few remarks about the
preacher boy without warning them specifically. But I
started to get nervous and my heart was beating as loudly
as a croaking frog. I would have to be careful. I wouldn't
want them to guess that I knew their secret. Then they'd
know I had a habit of hiding in the bushes and spying on
them, and that if anyone was perverted it was me.

I really didn't want to warn them, but I knew it was
the right thing to do, and doing the right thing was a kind
of desire line. I took a deep breath, hopped straight up
onto my feet, pushed the palm fronds aside, and
hollered, "Hi."

I startled the hell out of them.

Jennifer popped up and flicked her cigarette into the
pond as if I were going to get after her for smoking.
Karen fell over onto her back, then rolled onto her side
and scrambled to her feet.

"What are you doing here?" she said, slapping the dirt off her jeans as I walked around the pond.

"Feeding the ducks," I replied. I set my backpack down, nervously unfastened the buckle, and pulled out a plastic bag. "Stale bread," I said awkwardly. "For the ducks."

"You know who this guy is?" Karen said to Jennifer. But before she could answer Karen continued. "He's that loser who cheated off my science test a couple weeks ago."

"I didn't know that," Jennifer quickly replied. "But I did hear he might be a *ho-mo-sexual.*" She dragged the word out just like the preacher boy.

I jerked my head around. "What'd you call me?"

"On the way over here that preacher boy told us he thought you were one of *those* types he's all fired up about," Karen said.

"No," I said a little too sharply. "I'm not."

"Then why would he say so if you weren't?" Karen asked.

"Because he's lying," I said. "He's just stirring up trouble."

"Well, I don't know who to believe," she said coyly. "A cheater or a preacher? I'll have to give it some thought."

"Well, I'm *not* gay," I said.

"You already said that," Karen replied. "More than once."

Jennifer cracked up.

"So, what'd you say back to him?" I asked.

"I told him I'd have to ask you," she replied.

"Well, now you know I'm not."

"Hey, you don't have to sound so defensive about it. It really doesn't matter to me."

"Maybe he just thinks you're cute," Jennifer added.

When she said that, something inside me snapped. It was like suddenly everything had gone to another level. Now he had other people, two *dykes*, making fun of me.

"You can feed the ducks," I said abruptly, and tossed the bread to Karen. "I'll see you later, girls."

"Suit yourself," she replied, almost singing it.

I turned and followed my desire line directly toward school. As I walked I thought of a hundred different ways to hurt that kid. But mostly I just wanted to punch his lights out, get him down on the ground with my heel on his neck until he promised to never call me a fag again.

I must have looked wickedly pissed off as I climbed up and over the fence, because when he saw me coming he raised his hands above his head and said, "I know you're not a ho-mo. I'm just picking on you because you were the first guy I saw. It's nothing personal, so don't go off on me." Then he stuck out his chin and raised the Bible up over his head with both hands, as if he were holding the Ten Commandments.

As far as I was concerned, it just made him an easier

target. I hit him as hard as I could with a round river rock tucked inside my fist. Holding the rock was cheating. I knew this. And sucker-punching him was wrong too. But honestly, I didn't feel all that bad about it. I should have, but I didn't then, and I don't now either. After I drew my arm way back and threw the roundhouse with all I could get on it, I caught him just to the side of his head, on the temple. And when my fist cracked against his head he went over like he'd been struck by lightning. And he didn't move.

I thought I had killed him and I was panicked, because I had only wanted to smack some sense into him. But I was willing to settle for just scaring him into leaving me alone, leaving me out of his witch-hunt, or whatever. But I didn't want to kill him.

And I hadn't. Two things happened at the same time. He started to move, then got up onto his feet, which was a relief, and my fist began to throb, which got my full attention.

Then vaguely, but just vaguely, I had the feeling that I was playing into his hands, that I was scum and he was righteous. He knew it, too. And he played it to the hilt.

"I'm disappointed in you," he said, his voice suddenly full of hurt. "Jesus preaches against violence."

"Well, Jesus should preach about lying," I snapped back.

"Then just tell me what I want to know and I won't have to lie about you," he said.

"There aren't any homosexuals here," I said. "You're barking up the wrong tree."

"Come on," he groaned, and rubbed the lump on the side of his face. *"None?* It's like saying there are no blue-eyed kids here, or redheads. Get real. Every school this size has 'em. Believe me. This isn't the first school I've cleaned up. And this place has a reputation. What I don't understand," he said, "is why you're protecting them. Why can't they take care of themselves? Why do they need you lying for them?"

"Look," I said. "If any homosexual wants to stand up and be counted it's up to them. Not up to you."

"Or you to protect them," he said, poking the air with his finger. "Remember, Christ said, 'Come unto me, all ye that labor and are heavy laden, and I will give you rest.' Now tell me who they are. You'll feel better for it."

I could see I wasn't getting anywhere with him. I took a deep breath and got to the point. "Look, I'm just telling you not to go around calling me a homosexual to everyone when I'm not."

"Well," he said, sounding smarmy, "I just don't know that for sure, so I can't make that promise."

I could feel myself getting crazy all over again. I closed my eyes and actually sang to myself, "Sticks and stones will break my bones but names will never hurt me." It didn't help. I wanted to punch him on the other side of his head. Instead, I turned away and climbed back over the fence. He didn't say another word, but something he had said stuck with me.

As I walked off I began to think, maybe it wasn't up to me to protect the girls. Maybe it was up to the girls to protect themselves. Maybe I'm making something bigger out of this than what it was. Maybe I'm protecting them for my own selfish reasons, like wanting to be the only one who watches them naked on "Wild Kingdom" Thursdays. And really, was it any of my business to protect them?

Because Karen and Jennifer seemed together enough to defend themselves. And who's to say they wouldn't just march right up to the preacher boy and say, "Screw off, you little perv," then kick him in the nuts, and he'd go scurrying away like a three-legged dog.

Protecting the girls wasn't my fight.

Maybe it was.

I didn't know. But my hand was throbbing so much I couldn't think about it anymore. I could move all the fingers okay, and my wrist rotated just fine, it's just that it hurt to do it. Still, I figured nothing was broken so I went to the U-Tote-Em, bought a bag of ice, and chilled my hand down until it felt like I had frostbite.

Boxed In

That preacher boy was getting to me. The more I thought about it, the more I began to spend a lot of extra time looking in the mirror at my face. Baby face, really. I had always had a cute face. Long eyelashes. Little nose. Pudgy cheeks. Pink skin. When I was in sixth grade, kids thought I was in third grade. When I was in ninth grade, I looked like I was in sixth grade. I was concerned that I looked too feminine. It was bad enough being called Baby face. I definitely didn't want to graduate to Sweet boy.

Since that preacher boy had been telling other kids out on the gym field that I was a fairy, I felt they were looking at me funny. Maybe they were, maybe they weren't. For a while I wasn't sure. When I'd march back and forth along my desire line I'd try and catch someone pointing or staring, but they were all looking the other way. Still, I could just imagine what they were thinking: homo, faggot, queer.

And then it happened. A few days after my run-in with the preacher boy, I was walking up the hallway when I heard, "Hey, queer bait."

I whipped around but everyone in the hall had a
straight face. Then as soon as I turned back the other way
I heard it again. "Sweetie pie, wanna give me a kiss?"

I spun around, but again everyone had a straight face.
I knew it must have been someone in the back of the hall
about twenty feet away, because I could hear laughing.
But no one stepped forward, and I didn't wade into the
crowd looking for trouble. I just turned and got out of
there before the name-calling snowballed.

I had decided to grow a mustache, but after a week not
much was growing. It looked more like two blond eyelashes fluttering on my upper lip. And I began to do the
opposite of everything I thought was prissy. On the way
to school I made sure to drag my heels on the ground and
amble about with my shoulders rolled forward like the
Marlboro Man. I started cracking my knuckles. I knew I
was acting like an ass, but I couldn't help myself. The
thought of other kids thinking I was a faggot had gotten
to me. To top off my new image, I worked on walking
while dredging up a wad of spit from my throat and
launching it with so much force that it hit the ground and
bounced. That's what I was practicing when I saw the
church across the street from the school.

It surprised me because it was not what I expected. I
figured they'd put up some piece of junk. But this was a
simple, beautiful church. An old country church made of
hand-milled boards and probably built by the same peo-

ple who once worshipped in it. The preacher boy's father must have bought it lock, stock, and barrel, and had it moved overnight on a trailer. The church was almost square, with four tall windows down each side, and each big pane of glass hand-painted with green and white marble patterns. There was a small greeting porch up front where you could shake the preacher's hand after a service, and a wooden steeple on top to point your prayers directly toward God.

A concrete truck had arrived and they poured out a sidewalk from the street to the wooden front steps. When they just about had it finished, another truck arrived towing a trashy black-and-orange house trailer. Along the bottom edge of the trailer were painted little flames which reminded me of the yellow and red flame decals I used to put around the wheels on my model drag racers when I was a kid. The whole thing had the look of some traveling-carnival rig.

I had no problem with the church. But I thought it was kind of weird that the trailer, which they parked in the back of the church, was their home. It was so beat up, even dented, like when you squeeze a soda can too hard. I thought they would see the difference between how beautiful the church was and how dumpy they looked and try to clean themselves up. But no. The new church was the face they presented to the world, and behind it they were strictly trailer-trash.

The preacher boy and his brother were setting out a bunch of old busted-up lawn chairs and boxes of stuff as I stood on my desire line. I leaned indifferently against the school fence with my arms crossed, and spit. I was getting pretty good at it. I could hit what I was aiming for.

In the few days since I'd punched him, he'd been ignoring me when I passed by on my way to and from school. Now, when the preacher boy saw me standing there, he waved and put a big smile on his face. He untangled a bullhorn from a box of junk and raised it to his mouth. "I forgive you for punching me in the head," he shouted. I could hear the last word echo off the rows of houses in the development on the other side of the school. *Head, head, head.*

I spit again, hit a piece of broken glass, then turned to climb the fence.

"Why don't we become friends again?" he continued. *Again, again, again.*

I opened the fingers on my right hand, stretched them out, then slowly closed them into a fist. I didn't hit him hard enough, I thought to myself, then jumped down from the fence and headed back for the duck pond.

I had kept my pigs in the back yard for a few days while I built a little pen in the basement of the old golf-course clubhouse. I nailed up some chicken wire and gathered enough straw and sawgrass to cover the floor.

By now I had taken eight little pigs. They required a lot of work. I had to keep them and their pen clean, feed them, and keep them company.

I made eight leashes out of clothesline rope and looped them around their necks and took them for walks. They weren't good at walking in a straight line. It was more like walking an octopus. They'd slither around in circles, get knotted up with each other, and nearly strangle themselves. So it always took a long time until we inched our way to the duck pond. Then I'd tie them all up to a branch, and one by one dunk them into the pond and bathe them while they squealed as if I were drowning them. I kept telling them I was saving their little pink behinds, but they didn't trust me.

That afternoon I was herding the pigs back to the clubhouse when I heard the twins and Stephanelli.

Mal was shouting out, "Step . . . step . . . step, step, step!" Then I heard an "Oh, crap!" from Stephanelli. Then Mal hollered, "Put your back into it and stop your whinin'."

I looked out from a gap between some bushes and watched them for a minute. They were attempting to carry a huge wooden crate, the size of an old Volkswagen Bug, across the fairway. Mal was in front and Mike and Stephanelli were on the back corners. Mal grunted an order, they squatted down, picked up the crate, and staggered a few steps before Mal hollered, "Drop it!" Then they dropped it and fell over onto all fours, panting like dogs.

There they were, primitive men carrying their portable cave, having not yet invented the wheel.

"Hey, nature boy," Mal shouted when he saw me with the pigs. "How 'bout some help?"

"Yeah," Mike said. "We're dyin' here."

"Then no more M-80s," I hollered back.

"Christ, Walker," Mal replied, then spit to one side. "If I had wanted to hurt you I would've just taped an M-80 to your face. We were only having a little fun. Now come on. He who helps carry the clubhouse gets to join the club, now giddy-up and get your butt in gear."

Mike waved to me. "Give us a hand," he said.

"One minute," I yelled. "I'll be right back."

This was perfect, I thought. Nobody would mess with me if I was in a club with Mike and Mal. Calling me a fag would be like calling them fags. And Mal wouldn't settle for punching a guy just once. He'd punch him until he'd never open his mouth again.

I dragged the pigs back as best I could without snapping their heads off and got them down into their clubhouse pen. I tossed them a box of rotting vegetables I had taken out of the grocery-store trash. "Later, boys," I said, then turned and ran back to the fairway.

When I reached the box Mike turned to Stephanelli. "You go up front with Mal and let Walker work with me."

"Yeah, Stephanelli, you come up here with me and leave Nature boy and Mike back there. I need to make sure you aren't doggin' it. I swear I'm carrying this thing by myself."

"Aww," Stephanelli groaned as he ambled toward the front of the crate. "I'm not liftin' light."

Before he could say anymore Mal smacked him across the ear with his open hand.

"Oww," Stephanelli hollered and recoiled. "That's my bad ear."

"Now, don't give me any of your crying. Just lift. On the count of three," he ordered, "lift!"

We picked up the box and scuttled forward until Mal shouted, "Drop it!" We did.

Mike's Police Athletic League T-shirt was soaked through. I was already bent over at the waist fighting for air.

"Let's shake it!" Mal shouted. "Move 'em out!"

I bent over to lift my end. I felt as if I were picking up the edge of our garage. I could only manage to get it about a foot off the ground.

"Go!" he shouted. "Go. Go. Go . . ."

The four of us gritted our teeth and scurried another twenty feet before he shouted, "Drop it!"

The box was so heavy all I could do was grunt in agreement. When I got my breath I asked, "Where are we taking this?"

"Over there," Mike said, pointing to an old banyan tree about a hundred yards away. "Mal wants to hoist it up into the tree." He snatched up a handful of grass, chewed it, then spit it out like a sick dog.

"That's impossible," I remarked. "Up in the tree? This thing must weigh two hundred pounds."

"Well, he thinks it will fit up there."

"How's he plan to hoist it?" I asked.

"Rope," he said. He pointed to the crate. "We got it in the box."

"Where'd you get this?" I asked, and slapped the side of the crate.

"Stole it from a car lot."

Just then Mal jumped back onto his feet. "Break's over," he shouted. "Come on, you sweet boys. Quit your gabbin' and lift. I want this crate in the tree by dinner. Heave!" We lifted and waddled another twenty feet before he shouted, "Drop!"

"Can it be done?" I gasped, with the sweat dripping into my mouth.

"Don't know, but if Mal wants it done, believe me, it gets done."

"Suck it up, people, and lift!" Mall called out. "And step . . . step . . . step, right left. Step . . . step . . . step, right left. Drop."

I looked at Mike. He was hissing like a flat tire as he

pulled a long splinter out of the palm of his hand. He flicked the splinter away.

We staggered again and again across the fairway until we dropped the box under the banyan tree and leaned against it, panting and stretching out our fingers.

The trunk of the banyan was as squat as ten of us around. The enormous brown limbs spread out like wrinkled girders and were supported by columns of smaller trunks the size of my arms.

Mal pointed to the empty space about eight feet off the ground where the major limbs spread out from the crotch of the trunk. "That is where I want the box," he said.

Stephanelli whistled. "I saw a movie once," he said, shaking his head, "where some nut had a bunch of natives carry a riverboat through the jungles of Brazil. They were pulling it up a hill when it slipped and crushed nearly all of them." He suddenly looked over at Mal and flinched.

"You should be worried about me," he said coolly, and faked a slap at Stephanelli's ear. "That kind of dumb talk doesn't cut it, especially coming from a moron."

He turned to Mike. "Why don't you take Walker and go get something cold to drink from the U-Tote-Em. The movie critic and I will set up the ropes to get this thing ready to hoist."

. . .

By the time we returned, Mal and Stephanelli had wrapped the rope around the box as if it were a birthday present. At the top knot the rope continued up and looped over a higher branch and hung down to the ground.

After we had finished drinking the water, Mal was ready to get back to work. "Everyone, take off your shirts," he ordered. "Use 'em for gloves so you don't strip your hands. You three, work the rope. I'll lever it off the ground and lift from below. We'll see how that goes."

We pulled the rope until it was taut. Impossible, I thought. Our combined body weight wasn't enough to lift it off the ground.

"Pull!" Mal hollered. Then, "Breathe." Then, "Pull!"

The box slowly lifted, first a few inches, then a foot. Mal kept racing around the box, shoving rocks under the corners, pieces of dead trees and limbs. "Rest."

We relaxed our grip. The box remained steady on the small platform he built. We readjusted our shirts around the rope as high up as we could reach.

"Ready," he commanded. We tightened our grip. "Pull."

We did, with all our might, until our arms ached. Our bodies hung like sacks of sand, and the box rose, a few more inches, then another foot. "Rest."

Mal ran about gathering up more rocks and limbs,

anything that would help build the platform. When he had enough material he hollered, "Pull!"

We did, pulling down on the rope as though we were trying to ring the heaviest church bell ever cast. The only sound produced was the stretch of the rope, the groan of the limb overhead, and shushing leaves.

"Put some muscle into it! I want to get it up there today," he barked. "Now pull."

We gave it what extra we had. Mal shored it up and shouted, "Rest!"

My elbows ached from stretching out my arms. My hands burned.

"You have to give us a hand," Mike said to him. "We're wiped out. Besides, it feels more like we're going to pull the branch down before we raise the box up."

"Come on, you sweet boys," Mal said as he wrapped his hands around the rope. "I'll show you how a real man works."

The four of us pulled down on the rope and slowly the box lifted off its pile of rocks and branches. We kept adjusting our grip as inch by inch it lifted higher into the air until finally it was about eight feet off the ground. Mal cinched the rope off around the trunk. "Now," he said, "you three swing it back and forth until it fits into the crotch of the tree."

We did, and as the box swung over the Y of the tree trunk, Mal loosened the rope and it dropped in.

"Yes!" he hissed and pumped his fist. "I knew it would work."

It was wedged in crooked, but Mal figured we could level it out later.

"Before we leave there is one thing I want to settle right now. I've been thinking about what we should call ourselves," Mal said while squatting on the ground. "Los Cuates is a solid name. The Twins. Yin and yang. Good and evil. Love and hate. That's what we're all about."

He *had* been thinking about it. But before we could even consider Mal's idea, Stephanelli jumped right in.

"I got an idea too," he said. "I been thinking about it because of the box." He pointed at it.

"Yeah," Mal replied, and raised an eyebrow. "You have an idea? I think this is the first idea you've had this year."

"We'll call ourselves the Box," he said. "There are four corners to a box and four of us. If someone drops their corner, the other three are there to help." He brushed the hair out of his eyes and gave us all a big smile, with his head bobbing away like one of those goofy puppies in the back window of a car.

"If someone drops their corner," Mal replied, grinding out his words, "the other three are there to kick his butt."

"I like the Box," Mike said, trying to shape up the ideas. "The Twins are just us and them. The Box means all four of us."

Mal sort of set his face as though it was a ⟨
total irritation, then let the thought roll arou⟨
head until it mutated into his own idea. "It's like a four-
man coffin," he announced, and laughed. "I could go for
that."

Mike, then Stephanelli, then Mal turned toward me.
At first I didn't know what they were after, then I realized
it was my turn to say something. It was the first time I
understood that if one of us said, or did anything, the
others had to add to it. Had to agree, disagree, fight, or
join in. It was a box. Everything about us seemed to be
in rotation. Everything came in fours, with Mal being the
boss of the Box. He liked to either start a conversation,
and let everyone else chime in, or sum things up after we
all spoke our minds.

They were still waiting for me to speak. I glanced at
Mike. I glanced over at Mal. I studied their faces for answers as though I was cheating off the tests on either side
of me. I was still looking for that C, that comfort zone.
But their faces looked identical, were matching blank
sheets of paper with eyes, noses, and mouths. They were
the same height, the same square build, and wired the
same inside. Mike may have been a little nicer, but that
was part of his job. He worked the good-guy angle, and
Mal handled the bad-guy stuff. It was as if they had di-
vided the emotional turf between them.

"Box," I said, and gave it a thumbs-up. "I'm all for it."

Girl Talk

When I went into the animal lab the next morning Mr. Harvey was waiting for me.

"We gotta problem," he said, all businesslike. "The animal count is off. What gets delivered and what gets processed are not adding up. Do you know anything about some missing pigs?"

My throat tightened right up. There was no use fighting it. I had already told him I cheated, so I told him the rest.

"I rescued them," I said. "I've been setting them loose."

He gave me a puzzled look.

"In nature," I explained. "I've been setting them free out in the bushes."

He laughed. "You're off the wall," he said. "Even Greenpeace wouldn't do something this dumb. I bet they're all dead by now."

"Some," I said, managing a small lie. I was planning on setting them free once they got big enough, and I did figure that some of them might not make it. But I thought

if I told him I had them in a cage he'd make me bring
them back.

"Well, don't do it anymore," he said, not sounding
terribly angry. "I'm responsible for the animal count and
the more you take, the more trouble it is for me. Got it?"

"Okay," I said. "But you know what we are doing with
them is really awful."

"You're right," he said. "It's revolting. It's disgusting.
But if I dwell on it I won't be able to do my job, and then
I'll starve. So if it's a matter of the pigs having a good life
or me, then I pick me. We're not talking ideology here,
this is basic reality. If pigs gotta die for me to live, then
so be it."

"Got it," I agreed. I could tell he was heating up a bit,
maybe on the verge of a repeat of his survival-of-the-
dominant-species speech, which I wanted to avoid.

"And another thing," he said. "You keep skipping
class and for that you get another month of animal duty."

"Right," I said, without an argument.

"See you in class."

"Yes, sir," I snapped. What else could I do? I was
nothing but a little fish in the food chain.

No sooner did I sit down and get my biology book and
folder out of my backpack and onto my desk than Karen
turned toward me and said, "That preacher kid is telling
people the *ho-mo-sexual* sucker punched him."

Wendy, the girl who sat on the other side of me, laughed. The word was definitely out.

"Yeah," I said. "I know. I should have hit him harder."

"Well, you know what they say," she said smugly.

"No, I don't," I replied, about as deadpan as I could.

"He who protests the loudest only draws more attention to himself."

"Thanks for the bad Shakespeare," I replied, and turned away from her, but she wasn't finished with me.

"Only a loser with something to hide would let that guy get to him."

I was totally pissed off. Here she was, baiting me! She could only be this smug if she thought no one could know about her and Jennifer. But *I* knew, and I was now aching to say so. I felt like standing on my lab desk and pointing at her and shouting, She's the gay one and I'm not, now leave me alone. That fantasy consumed me for about half the class while I scribbled aimlessly in my folder. By the time I calmed down and began to think sensibly it dawned on me that she was relieved I was drawing all the attention, that I was running cover for her, while she and Jennifer could stay a secret. And realizing this made me feel something for her, like when I watch those wild-animal shows on TV and a pack of jackals have separated the weak one from a herd of kudu or something and are snapping at its legs until they bring it down and lunge for the throat. That's the kind of fear she must have, I thought. When she looks at us, she sees nothing but jackals.

But just when I was feeling that I should protect them in some way, defend them, she turned toward me at the end of class and said in a very nasty tone, "You can't take it, can you?"

And I just looked at her and thought, You don't know the half of it. But I said, "Yeah, it bothers me to be called a queer when I'm not." That was about as direct as I could put it.

"Did you ever notice how other people can figure things out about you before you see it for yourself?" she said piously.

"No," I said.

"Then maybe you should pay attention to what people say about you," she suggested. "You might learn something."

Before I said something I'd regret, I just turned away from her and ambled out the door, down the hall, and toward my desire line, where I let fly a wad of spit. She knew what I was going through with the preacher boy, and she didn't care. She'd let me be called gay boy all day long, in front of the whole school, the whole town, the world, as long as she didn't have to step forward. She was the one who was *really* scared. She was the one who couldn't take it. And then I had to smile. I just remem-

bered that it was a Thursday, time for another episode of
"Wild Kingdom."

I went to the pond early. I wanted to get close enough
to hear what they talked about, without them seeing me.
I climbed a tree that arched over the pond and found a
good spot to sit, about thirty feet up. I began to wonder
if I could hear them if they were below me so I fished
around in my pocket for some pennies. The air was dead
still. I threw the pennies one at a time into the pond.
When they hit the water I heard the *blup, blup,* loud and
clear. I looked down at the water. With the sun setting
and the shadows reaching across the pond, and the
ducks settling down, it seemed I could make out the
image of the boy who had supposedly drowned long ago.
Before the sinkhole was called the duck pond it had
actually been called the snake pit. Guys used to go down
there and swing from a rope tied up in a tree and drop
into the pond. There were no ducks then. Just water
moccasins. One guy took a swing out on the rope, let go,
and from the story I heard, when he hit the water about
a dozen moccasins went straight for him. How no other
kid had ever been attacked I don't know, but that's how
these stories go, full of holes. The kid thrashed around
and the water boiled as they bit him all over. He never
made it back to the bank. He slipped down into the
water. His friends didn't try and save him. They didn't

throw him a rope. Not even a branch. They just ran away and vowed to keep quiet. They were scared. Finally, one of them couldn't keep the secret any longer and went to the police. State scuba divers were called, but they couldn't locate the body. The divers never even reached the bottom of the sinkhole. They thought maybe the pond linked up with a network of other tunnels eroded in the limestone, and the body may have been pulled along by a warm current that took it out to the Atlantic Ocean. His family nailed a small wooden cross to a tree and wrote his name on it and the date of his death. Afterward, the county pest control came in and poisoned the sinkhole and killed off all the snakes. Eventually the poison filtered out and the ducks found the place and took it over. When I discovered the pond you could still see where an old frayed piece of rope was knotted high up around one of the upper oak boughs and part of the cross was still nailed to the tree, with a few plastic roses tucked behind the wood, the rest scattered on the ground.

Now I realized I was in the tree where the swinging rope had been tied. I thought I could throw myself into the water, like some human wishing-well offering, and join that kid down at the bottom of the hole. If I was dead, everything would go away. But I knew that no amount of wishing was going to solve anything for me. I was on my own.

Karen arrived first. Then Jennifer. They didn't undress. They just sat in the dark, back to back, holding each other up. They passed a cigarette between them and with each drag it glowed as if it were a firefly. I waited.

Suddenly they seemed to pick up in the middle of a conversation.

"What if we just told people and got it over with?" Jennifer asked.

"No way," Karen shot back. "No way in hell."

"Well, I already feel like I'm in *hell*," Jennifer said.

"Well, you aren't," Karen said impatiently. "Real *hell* would be your parents finding out. Real *hell* would be my dad going ballistic. Real *hell* would be everyone at school looking us over and calling us all kinds of dyke names."

"But I'm in a private *hell*," Jennifer said.

"Well, as far as I'm concerned," Karen said, "I'd rather have my own private *hell* than the public *hell* that would come with being outed. At least I'm the boss of my private hell, and that I can live with."

"Well, what do we do?" Jennifer asked. "Just sit tight and let it blow over?"

"Things like this never blow over," Karen said. "They just blow up."

"You depress me," Jennifer said. "One day the world means nothing to you and you give it all the finger. The next day the slightest concern sends you over the edge."

"Well, that's just the way it is," she snapped. "Right now there is not a lot of fun in my life. Every day I have to wonder, who is going to find out about us, and who is going to screw up my life. And I'd rather not wait for someone to screw it up for me. I'd rather screw it up myself. It's my life, and I'll be damned if I'm going to sit back and wait for someone to mess it up for me."

Jennifer didn't say a word after that. They just sat there in the dark. I don't know for how long, because I didn't dare move my arm to look at my watch. Finally Karen stood up. "Let's go," she said. "I'm cold."

Tag Team

A few days later things started to go downhill fast.

Mike and Mal had leveled out the box and the four of us were sitting inside. They had gone to a carpet discount warehouse and picked up a huge stack of free out-of-style carpet samples. They had nailed them to the inside of the box—floor, walls, and ceiling—with long nails that stabbed through the wood so that from the outside the box looked like a square porcupine. Birds wouldn't even land on it, and on the inside, since it was padded, I don't think anyone could hear you even if you screamed. They had made hinges out of carpet scraps for the top of the door and propped the bottom open a few inches with a stick. What little air drifted through the opening was humid, and before long we were breathing in each other's exhale. It was stifling hot and the sweat was running down our faces and drenching our shirts.

The sun had already set. It was dark outside, and so dark inside the twins had brought a battery-powered camping lamp for light. Each one of us was sitting cross-legged in his corner of the box. We just seemed to be staring at each other with nothing much to say, as if we were seeds, soaking up the light, waiting to sprout into the exact same plant.

Then Mal started up. "I've been thinking," he said. "As a club, we need rules. Dos and Don'ts. When you look at your buddy you don't want to be confused. That's why you have rules, to be one mind, one body. You don't want to look at your buddy and think, What's on his mind?

"Also, we need an initiation process that sets up some trust among us. What I think is, everyone has to lead us into and out of something bad, something dangerous, forbidden. And if we all get through it, then we end up like blood brothers."

Stephanelli brightened. "Like in the Boy Scouts, like when you slice the tip of your finger and let your blood mix with the blood of your friend."

Mal sprang forward and slapped him across the face. Stephanelli's head snapped back and hit the wall with a muffled thud.

"What century are you living in?" Mal yelled. "You talk like you belong to the AIDS brigade. Share blood? I'd rather share blood with a rat!"

Stephanelli squinted through his wet eye. "It's just an idea, man. You don't have to go ballistic and poke my eye out."

"And you don't have to be such a bonehead. But you are."

"Don't call me names, man."

"It's not a name if it's the truth."

I watched them snipe back and forth, and wondered if they'd ever stop or if the combination of Mal's anger and Stephanelli's sniveling was like a perpetual-motion machine that just kept pouring out a steady dose of trash talk.

Finally Mike was fed up with them too. "Cut the crap," he said. "Let's get to the point. Everyone has to give something up. Stephanelli, what's it going to be."

"Yeah, wise guy," Mal said to Stephanelli. "You heard the rules. And since you're the smart mouth that named us the Box, then you go first. And it better be good."

Stephanelli glanced over at Mal and shrank all the way back and wedged himself into his corner before he spoke. "I think we oughta go mess with that preacher boy's head," he said in a malicious whisper. "I been thinking that we ought to spray our club tag on the church."

"And what tag might that be, wonder boy?" Mal asked.

"I got that worked out too," he replied. "A dice. Like a dice with four dots on it as if you rolled it and it came up a four. You know, the Box is square, the dice is square. There are four of us, so four dots on the dice. Get it?"

Mal dove on Stephanelli, pinned him down, then kissed his eye. He pounded on his head with his knuckles. "That's amazingly brilliant. How did a moron like you come up with such a good idea? Did you cheat? Did you read someone's mind? Did you get a brain transplant? Suddenly you've become some kind of gifted and talented moron coming up with one whole idea every day."

Stephanelli grinned like a big ol' dog. He fell over onto his side and beamed. His wretched teeth flashed like a set of twisted pinking shears. His head bobbed with canine bliss.

Mal smiled. "Brilliant," he repeated. "You sick genius. This is why I love you. Well, what are we waiting for? Let's go."

We bought the paint in a hardware store, even though it was after dark and there was a sign on the spray-paint case that read, "Not for sale to minors." We just put the tall cans of black and yellow and pink up on the counter, paid cash, and walked out the door.

It didn't take long to reach the church. It was the same as going to school. The lights were off inside, so we figured the preacher family was in the house trailer out back eating out of cans with plastic sporks. It was a dark night but the church was so white it glowed from its own light, and against it we stood out like hand shadows on a screen.

"You two take the front," Mal whispered. "We'll take the side."

Stephanelli and I tiptoed up onto the front porch. We were under the overhang, which covered us with a faint shadow.

"This is awesome," he said and began to shake the cans of paint as if he were some kind of spastic Mariachi.

"Quiet," I whispered.

"Chill," he replied. "I done this a hundred times."

I had begun to like Stephanelli and I knew it was because he was the one being kicked around and I was the one almost kicked around, and next in line to be kicked around. I was like him. Or almost. He was really Mal's pal. And I had pretty much paired up with Mike. But they had a two-tier social ladder. The twins were on top and Stephanelli and I were on the bottom. Even now they were around the side of the church doing something they wouldn't tell us about.

"I just got another incredible idea," Stephanelli said excitedly. "I'm gonna do two dice. A pair of snake eyes. Do you get it?"

"Yeah," I said. "So let's get going."

"Well, give Picasso some room."

I stepped back and he began to spray with the black, working up the three-dimensional outlines of the dice.

"What do you think the twins are doing?" I asked.

"Pink triangles, I guess," he said. "*You* know how crazy that preacher kid is." He shook the can and sprayed some more. "When he sees the homo tag on his church he'll go berserk."

I could just imagine it. He'll be standing out on the church lawn with his bullhorn just waiting for me to show up so he can put on a show. Painting the dice on the church was bad enough, but no one could say just *who* painted them. But the pink triangles will be pointed right at me, just like his finger as he hollers, "Ho-mo! Ho-mo! Ho-mo!"

I leaned over the porch railing to spit when suddenly the church door flung open and Stephanelli hollered out "Whooa" as though he had seen a ghost, and jumped back onto my feet. Of course, I was scared witless because I knew I was doing something dead wrong, and because I was so totally afraid my legs went to jelly. At that moment I tried to run but because Stephanelli was standing on my feet I just lunged forward and fell off the porch and sprawled onto the concrete sidewalk. Stephanelli bolted over the porch rail and took off, and by then the preacher boy's dad was standing over me.

"Oh no you don't," he growled when I tried to hop up,

and he stomped down onto my left hand with his work
boot. He was furious, and it felt as though a corner of the
church had pinned my hand. From where I was, on all
fours on the sidewalk, and from where he was, standing
on my hand, we both could make out the unfinished dice
on the church door.

"Why did you do that?" he shouted.

I didn't know what to say.

He squatted down and picked up the black spray can
Stephanelli left behind.

"Well, say something," he said angrily. "Speak up."

I tried to pull my hand away but couldn't get it loose.

He reached down and grabbed the back of my T-shirt
and tried to raise me up to get a closer look at my face,
but the neck of my shirt ripped and he stumbled. Instead
of lifting up his foot, he just pivoted all his weight on it,
which ground my palm further across the concrete.

"I didn't do it," I said. "Now get off of my hand."

"Liar," he shot back. "Who are you?"

I didn't reply. All I wanted to do was run.

"Are you some school kid? You the one who hit my
boy?"

I was hoping the preacher boy wouldn't come out and
recognize me. But he wouldn't have been able to identify
me because just then his dad began to spray black paint
all over my head. "You . . . creep," he growled, spraying
and shaking the can.

"I didn't want to do this," I insisted and stretched my face away from the paint, but I could still feel it running into my ear and down my neck.

"What kind of lame excuse is that?" he hollered.

"You're breaking my hand," I cried out. "Now get off."

"What's your name?"

I heard the hiss first, then saw the burning fuse, then a flash of light along with an explosion. As soon as the first one went off, the preacher jerked back and raised his foot. Mal stepped out around the corner and tossed another M-80. It went off overhead.

I was on my feet and across the lot in seconds.

"Hey, come back here," he shouted. "I'm calling the cops."

I hooked left across the street, scrambled over the fence, and jumped down and kept going until I was a good ten blocks away. Then I slowed down and stood behind an old royal palm and pulled the T-shirt over my head. I wiped my face as best I could, then turned it inside out and put it back on. I kept looking for car lights, but none showed up. No cops, and no preacher dad. I stepped out from behind the tree and kept running.

When I got home I went in through the back door to the garage. I found the mineral spirits and a rag and stared into the side mirror on my dad's car. I looked like some sweaty coal miner who just got off the night shift.

The Next Day

The morning after the church fiasco I woke up like anyone else. Showered like anyone. Ate like anyone. And
disliked myself maybe more than most. I was sick. I was
a coward. I couldn't stand up for myself. I was caving in
to other people's bad ideas. Things were working against
me because I was working against myself. There was a
gap between what I wanted to say and what I said; what
I wanted to do and what I did; what I thought I felt and
what I really did feel. And that gap kept getting wider.
It's like I was getting lost in my thinking. I started out
going in one direction and ended up in another. There
was no straight line to it. It was as though I stepped out
of my house thinking I was going to the library and
ended up at a book-burning rally. Or looked at a bird and
called it a fish. I know I was fixated on the way things
decayed, but I never thought I would be the one falling
apart.

I tried to line up the facts in my mind. The preacher
boy had singled me out and had me acting like some
kind of Neanderthal Man, spitting, walking with my

knuckles dragging the ground, and going out on a spray-painting mission like some dog peeing on lampposts to mark his territory. So what was my next move? What was the right thing to do, before I did the wrong thing? "Just suck it up and don't let anything bother you," I said to myself. "Let him call you names, let the girls make fun of you, let everyone at school think what they will, and just mind your own business and eventually it will all go away."

That's what I told myself in the morning. And I kept repeating it to myself as I walked to school. And for a while I actually half believed that nothing anyone said about me could get through.

Then I rounded a bend and saw the big pink triangle emblazoned on the side of the church with the words, HOUSE OF HO-MO written across the top. Right away I felt my resolve slipping. The preacher boy stood on the sidewalk with the bullhorn screwed up in front of his mouth. He was like a sniper sitting up on a little hill just waiting for me to come into range, and when he saw me coming down the line he nearly hopped up and down with hatred.

"Here he is now," he boomed out to the half dozen or so kids who were also walking to school. "He's the one." *One, one, one.* He stood in front of the church, pointing at me, then pivoting like a pinball flipper to point at the triangle, then back again at me. "This is a house of

God," he hollered. "And this man has done the work of the devil."

"Way to go, Walker," a kid cracked as he passed by. "Why didn't you just torch the place?"

When he said that, I did feel regret. It was a shame to see the pink triangle and the half-formed dice and the nasty writing, because the church was so beautiful and everything else—the scrubby fields, the rusty chain-link fences, the trashy house trailer, the school—was so ugly. Now the church was as ugly as everything else.

"Hey!" he hollered, waving the red leather Bible up over his head as though he could stir the air into a tornado of God's cleansing power. "Though your sins be as scarlet, they shall be as white as snow. That if thou shalt confess with thy mouth, thou shalt be saved!"

I kept walking and all along I was talking to myself. Nothing he says is bothering me. Nothing. Nothing. Nothing. I kept repeating the word, nothing, as if it were a brick I could build into a wall between us.

Nothing. Nothing. Nothing.

And then he started with the names again. He was kicking my ass, and he knew it.

"Hey, closet case," he yelled. "Hey, fruit loop. You can't stop me from doing God's work. No amount of gay evil can defeat God's word."

That was it. I picked up a handful of rocks and began to whip them at him as hard as I could. A few kids stopped to watch me but I didn't care. I had lost it. He dodged the first two, then turned and ran around the far corner of the church. When I couldn't see him anymore I dropped the rocks in my hand and turned away.

Then as soon as I began to march toward the animal pens, his head popped out from behind the building, *"Have a nice day!"* he boomed.

I wanted to kill him.

The familiar smell in the lab was actually a relief from being outside. The pig cage was empty. They had been prepared overnight. I now had about a hundred white mice to manage. They were easy. I cleaned the bottom of their cage, changed the paper litter, gave them fresh water and food, and checked out. Usually I gave them a little pep talk about sacrificing themselves for the greater good of mankind, but since I wasn't doing so well for myself, I didn't think I could help them either.

When I took my seat in biology class Karen was waiting for me. It had come to the point that every time she saw me she had to make some smart-ass comment. Had to say something to just see how I was holding up. The preacher boy was kicking my butt on one side, and she was needling me from the other.

"How'd you hurt your hand?" she asked.

I had it wrapped in a thick gauze bandage after the preacher dad had scraped the skin off the palm and ground his Georgia boot heel across my knuckles. "It's still swollen from when I hit that preacher kid," I replied. "He had a hard head."

"How come you have black paint in your ear?" she asked.

"How come you keep asking me questions?"

"Because," she said slowly, deliberately, "I think you must have painted the church up."

"Think again," I said. "It wasn't me."

"Well, who else would it be?" she asked. "You're the guy he's been after. So it figures you're the guy who's fighting back."

"What's it to you, anyway?" I said. "The kid is a jerk. He just wants me to help him railroad the queers out of school."

"So what are you going to do?" she asked.

I watched her every gesture, her eyes, the corners of her mouth, her smooth forehead for some little evidence of fear, but there was nothing. A poker face. *Nothing* had gotten to her. She was perfectly composed, and waiting for me to make the next move, to tell her something she was dying to know.

"It's none of his business," I said.

Even though I didn't see fear in her, I did see relief. Definitely. Some pressure had been let off. She seemed to deflate a bit, like a tire. I figured she found out what she wanted to know without asking me a direct question.

"You're right," she said, suddenly sincere, as if we had been friends for a long time. "It's none of anyone's business."

Except mine, I thought to myself. And I was sick of the whole thing.

Sinkhole

In the afternoon I marched over to the Box. I climbed up the knotted rope and crawled inside. It was hot. I propped the door open and waited for them to show. It was my turn to give something up, tell them something that would make me part of the Box. I knew there was only one thing to give them that they would want to hear. It was the same thing everyone wanted to hear. Who were the homosexuals? The answer was slowly but surely working its way forward from the dark ledge in my brain. No matter how hard I labored to keep my secret back there, it was coming, had been coming for a while, and now it was just on the tip of my tongue.

After the guys climbed the rope and crawled into their corners the talk started off easy enough. I took some ribbing for having the preacher dad flatten my hand. We laughed over the M-80s scaring him off, and high-fived Mike and Mal for the HOUSE OF HO-MO label on the church. While Stephanelli was trying to talk us into returning so he could finish his dice, I just floated along, bided my time.

Then Mal got right to the point. "Enough of last night," he announced, and nodded toward me. "It's Walker's turn. What's it going to be, partner? Ante up to be part of the Box."

I looked at Mike. He had locked on to Mal's lead. "What do you have in the back of your mind you'd like to share with us?" Mike asked. "I know you got something in there for show-and-tell." He reached forward and tapped on my head as if he could shake it loose. "Now, come on. You can't let Stephanelli outclass you."

"Spit it out, Walker," Mal said, picking up steam. "Something juicy. We didn't let you into the Box just because we thought you were a nice guy. We know that deep inside you're an asshole like the rest of us."

"Come on, man," Stephanelli coaxed. "The church thing was easy to come up with."

"You can trust us," Mal replied. "We're all brothers in this Box."

They leaned forward, waiting. I felt like some old gold miner, ready to kick the bucket, and with my last words was supposed to give up the secret location of the lost treasure.

"Sorry," I said. "I can't think of a thing." And inside me, what I knew was just aching to cut loose.

Mal turned to me. "Walker," he said menacingly, "just the fact that you don't have *anything* to give up means you do know *something*. But since you don't want to spit it out right now I'll give you a little breathing room to work on it while I set a positive example."

I shrugged and looked away, thinking that maybe I wouldn't have to give up the girls. Maybe I could just be an idiot like Stephanelli and never have to say anything serious. I could just tag along for the ride, blurt out something stupid every now and again, and keep anything too dangerous just under the surface.

"I know who the real flamer is," Mal said suddenly, and let that float out there for a moment.

For an instant I thought he knew what I knew, and I wondered how he had found out.

"Well, who?" Stephanelli asked. "Who be the 'mo?"

"Walker," Mal said, and pointed toward me. "Sadly, the fourth corner of the Box is a swish."

"No way," I shot back, defending myself.

"Way," Stephanelli kicked in. "Why else would you be hanging around the golf course playing daddy with pigs?"

"I'm trying to save them," I said.

"Yeah, like Rebecca of Sunnybrook Farm," Mal continued. "Like I said, fag behavior. Just like that preacher boy says."

"I'm not," I replied. "And that freak knows it."

"I don't know why he'd lie," Mal mused. "Him being a Man of God and all."

"He's a sham," I said. "He's just out on a witch-hunt."

"Well, if you aren't the fag, tell us who is. Because if you're protecting fags, you must be one. And I'm not the only one who thinks this way. Mike and Stephanelli and I and the whole school are scratching our butts wondering why that preacher boy is after *you* and nobody else."

"Yeah," Mike said. "What does he know about you that we don't know?"

"Give it up," Mal insisted, looking right at me. "And make it good. I saved your sorry ass last night and you did nothing but run. You owe me, shit, you owe us all. If you're the fag, then rat your own self out and deliver the goods."

By the time he finished I was aching to hand over the one thing I could, and in one swipe get the preacher and Mike and Mal and Stephanelli and everyone at school off my back.

Since I knew I was going to say it, I figured I might as well play it to the hilt. "Okay, I know who some fags are," I said, going straight for it. "That preaching freak is just playing guessing games, but I know the real story."

I got a huge rush when I said that, and I got off on watching Mike and Mal and Stephanelli suddenly lurch forward like hungry dogs just waiting for me to feed them.

"The fags aren't guys, they're *dykes*," I said, letting it all air out. "I saw them doing it at the duck pond."

"Who?" Mal asked.

"Karen Spencer and Jennifer Owet," I said. And just so Mal wouldn't forget what a good guy I was, I made it sound about as lurid as I could. "It was awesome. X-rated. And I can show you where they get it on."

I was a hit. Mal fell over backwards, whooping like a maniac, drumming his hands on the carpeted floor. "Dykes on the duck pond," he hollered. "Lordy!"

Stephanelli just leered from ear to damaged ear as he made smooching sounds in the air. I wasn't sure what he was doing, but it must have been vulgar in some way.

"We have hit the jackpot," Mike announced, and gave me a buddy punch on the shoulder. "Nice work, Walker."

Odd, how much better I felt. The only thing I could think of was that I was like a person who had just flown into a rage and said something he never meant to say. But no one ever mistakenly says something like that. This was no slip of the tongue. No accident. I gave them up in order to save my own ass. Pure and simple.

"When is *show* time?" Mal asked.

"Thursday night," I replied. "You just have to be there, and hope they get the feeling."

"I got the *feeling* right now," Stephanelli sang.

I had a different feeling.

Before and After

It was just a thought. Like one of those thoughts you have that you don't act on, that later you realize was not just an everyday thought. But a message. A telegram. A wake-up call from God, or whatever you want to call it. I was in the cafeteria during Thursday lunch when I saw Karen and Jennifer sitting alone at a table. The words popped into my head as if the preacher boy had his megaphone pressed against my ear: Walker, you asshole, you just served them up.

It was a pretty strong thought and right then I should have walked over to them and said, "I know what you do every Thursday night at the duck pond, but don't do it tonight. Go somewhere else." But I didn't have the guts to say it to them. And I didn't have the guts to deal with Mike and Mal if we sat at the pond all night and saw nothing but sleeping ducks.

I just turned around and sucked it up. It's not your fight, I said to myself. It's not up to you to protect them. They're big girls, they can handle it themselves. Besides, I thought, what they don't know won't hurt them.

That didn't make me feel any better. It just gave me something to say to myself as I walked out the door and headed for class.

I met the guys at the duck pond just before sunset. Mal was in full military camouflage. Mike wore black and Stephanelli wore a Mickey Mouse T-shirt. I brought my camo tarp and we set it up like a hunter's duck blind, closer to the pond than I had ever set it before. Mal wanted to be close so we could see and hear all the action. We cut slits in the fabric so we could peek out. Then we sat down to wait.

I kept hoping they wouldn't show up, or that we'd be too loud and they'd hear us in advance and stay away. But Mal insisted on silence and he punched Stephanelli each time he giggled or uttered a sound.

The moon was rising when Karen arrived. We leaned forward on our knees and stared through the peepholes. She spread out the blanket and arranged the candles. It had always been so beautiful to watch her do those simple things, but now they seemed repulsive, as though everything she did was going to be held against her in some way, as if lighting candles from now on would be called fag behavior.

Then we all heard Jennifer shuffling through the brush.

"Over here," Karen called.

Jennifer stepped out of the darkness and into the flickering light. She held a bouquet of black-eyed Susans in her hand. "The moon is fabulous," she said. "I could see to pick these."

Now it seemed like picking flowers in the moonlight was fag behavior.

"You're late," Karen said. "I've been waiting."

"Band," she replied as an explanation. "It ran late." Band was now fag behavior.

Karen reached for the flowers.

"No. I thought I'd float them on the pond," Jennifer said, and knelt down at the water's edge. One by one, she carefully lowered the stems into the water, as if she were threading a needle, so that each blossom drifted across the surface. "I wish we had thousands," she said. "We could cover the entire pond. We could sleep on them."

Suddenly one blossom went straight down. Jennifer squealed. "Did you see that? Something snatched it. A fish or something."

"I told you I thought there was something down there," Karen said knowingly. "I'm not going swimming. It's like the Creature from the Black Lagoon is under there waiting for us."

"You just don't like water," Jennifer remarked, dipping her hands into the pond and rinsing the dirt off. She sat back onto the blanket, wiggled out of her backpack, and unzipped it. "Look!" she cried out, and held up a bottle of wine, then two plastic cups. "And," she added proudly, "I already popped the cork."

Suddenly wine was a fag drink.

Karen held the cups while Jennifer bit down on the top half of the cork to work it open. It squeaked back and forth.

"You're going to pull your teeth out," she warned. "I knew someone who did that once. And their tooth got stuck in the side of the cork. It was gross."

The cork popped and Jennifer poured the wine.

Don't kiss, I kept saying to myself, as if I could steer their actions telepathically. Just talk. But after they drank a sip of wine they kissed. Fag behavior. Stephanelli tapped me on the shoulder. I tilted my head toward him. He gave me a thumbs-up and grinned so widely his teeth glowed like a handful of crystals. The three of them in a row looked like perverts staring through glory holes in bathroom stalls. And there I was, the pervert of the Peaceable Kingdom, handing the girls over so no one would ever call me gay again.

I looked back at the girls. It was different when I was watching them by myself. I knew what *I* was thinking, and feeling. But when I glanced over at Stephanelli, Mike, and Mal it was different. It was sick. I was sick.

Don't undress, I thought. Whatever you do, don't undress. Almost immediately, Karen pulled her shirt up and unsnapped her bra.

I had fallen into a sinkhole, and I knew it. It was as if at one moment I was standing on solid ground and the next I was sinking straight down to hell, not the hell that the preacher boy wanted for me. The hell with dancing flames and hot coals and a devil with horns and a pitchfork, but my own hell—the kind you make for yourself when you totally go against what you know is the right thing to do. But it was too late to turn back.

Jennifer lit a candle and turned on the radio. Then in one motion she bent forward at the waist and pulled her T-shirt over her head. She straightened up, reached behind her back, and unhooked her bra. She hung it and her shirt over a branch that crossed above the blanket. She stood that way, naked from the hips up, her nipples erect, as she lit a cigarette.

Karen undressed from the bottom up. She sat on the blanket and untied her shoes, set them aside, and stood. She unbuckled the top button on her jeans, pulled down the zipper, and tugged the waist of the jeans down over her hips. Then with her left foot she held down the hem of her right pants leg as she stepped out, then repeated the move for the other. She hooked her thumbs on either side of her panties and peeled them down.

I was just hoping that everyone would keep quiet, would just let the girls do what they wanted to do and keep their mouths shut, when Mal hollered out, "Hey, girls." He stood up and bounded over the tarp. "Why settle for less when you could have the best," he declared, and strolled toward them like God's gift to women, as he pulled his shirt up over his head.

Stephanelli jumped forward, tripped over the tarp, and crashed into the bushes like a crazed, howling lunatic.

Jennifer screamed. Karen yelled, "Get out of here, asshole!"

Stephanelli popped up, saying, "Dykes. Wow. Dykes."

"Aw, come on," Mal said. "Don't get dressed. We could just be gettin' started." He grabbed Jennifer's shirt and bra off the tree limb.

"Leave us alone, you creep," Karen said as she snatched up her clothes and pressed them against her body. "And take that idiot with you." She must have meant Stephanelli.

Mike leaped over the tarp and out into the clearing.

"Oh, shit," Jennifer cried, and bolted.

"Aww, don't run," Mal said. "The fun's just getting started."

"Come back," Karen called out. "Wait for me." Then she turned and ran off behind Jennifer.

Mike and Mal were whooping it up and Stephanelli was rolling across the ground, braying like an asthmatic mule.

"Walker," Mal called toward me. "Come on out. They're gone. Walker. Damnit, Walker, where'd you go?"

I could hear him but I had already turned the other way and was hacking through the bushes. It was dark and I wasn't sure where I was. The branches scratched me as I kept swinging my arms out in front of my face while driving one foot down in front of the other.

When I reached a clearing I waded out into the middle of a field of tall grass and dropped down onto my knees. I closed my eyes. I had always pictured myself as one of the good people in the Peaceable Kingdom. But not anymore. I was the snake in the garden. I could hear the preacher boy's harangue ringing in my ear: You serpents! you vipers! How ye escape the damnation of hell?

I stood up. The moon was so low and bright my shadow looked like the needle on a compass. I followed it over to the abandoned clubhouse. I picked my way down into the basement where I kept the pigs. They were asleep.

"Come on," I said, and ran a stick back and forth across the wire cage. "Time to go. Nature's calling."

I figured if I couldn't save the girls I couldn't save the pigs. They were both better off without me helping them. A few at a time, I carried them outside and set them down on the ground. When I had them all gathered I said, "It's survival of the fittest pigs." Then I chased them off. They ran squealing and snorting through the brush and calling out in all directions.

"Good luck," I said behind them. "Remember, winners make history. Losers make lunch."

Nailed

I spotted the first one on Friday. Before I crossed the street I saw it. One of the baby pigs had been hit by a car. It was a bloody, bloated mess and had been knocked off the road and up against a little hill of trash. I brushed the flies away with a Burger King bag and picked it up. I carried it to an abandoned irrigation well and dropped it inside. One down, I thought to myself, seven more to go. Then I headed for the Box. I wasn't skipping school, for once. It was an official holiday.

At first I planned to never go back there again. But then I thought I needed to go one more time, just to quit. I didn't want to see them again, but I had some unfinished business.

When we were all gathered, Mal got right to the point.

"Hey, Walker," he said. "You really turned me on last night. You know what I did when I went home?"

"No," I answered. I really didn't want to know. I glanced at Mike. He was smiling. He knew. I glanced at Stephanelli. He knew.

"I started to think," Mal said proudly. "I thought I'd

qualify for the Box by telling the preacher boy who some *real* fags are."

He paused to study my face for a reaction.

"You wouldn't tell him about me?" I asked.

"Oh, no," he replied. "I wouldn't rat you out. You're a part of the Box. After last night, even though you ran off, you're one of us."

"This is going to be awesome," Mike said. "Once the preacher boy smells blood he'll drive those dykes into the ground."

"I don't think you should tell him," I said. "It'll get back that I'm the one who told."

"No it won't," he said.

"It will," I replied.

"What's wrong?" Mal asked. "You should be a happy camper. I plan to keep the preacher from telling everyone you're a homo-queer-faggot, but somehow you don't look real pleased." He leaned forward and took nothing but pleasure in knowing I was squirming inside.

"I'm not pleased," I said. "I made a mistake last night. But not anymore. I quit."

"You can't," Mike said.

"Well, I just did."

"We *own* you," he insisted.

"How do you figure that?" I asked.

"I'm not going to tell the preacher *who* ratted out the girls," Mal said. "But Mike will. And this is why we *own* you. Because we figure you won't like it when the preacher boy is out on the front yard hollering, *'Walker* told me Karen and Jennifer are the dykes!' "

"Think about it," Mike said. "You're more interested in saving your ass than you are in saving theirs. And this is how I'm qualifying for the Box. If you stay I'll keep *your* secret. But if you leave, I'll give it away. Your choice."

"I'm leaving," I replied.

I turned and crawled toward the opening.

"I wouldn't do that if I were you," Mal sang in a false sweet voice. I kept crawling.

"This is it for me," I said. "I'm out of here."

"Hey, you can't just go," Mike warned me and shifted to block the door. "You're a member now. We're a Box now. Mal, Stephanelli, me, and you."

I turned to Stephanelli. "What nasty shit do they have on you?" I asked.

"What do you mean?" he replied and hunched up his shoulders.

"I mean, it's clear that I screwed up. I thought I could hang around with you guys and keep the preacher boy off my back. I didn't think it was going to cost me like this. But what about you, Stephanelli? Why would you hang out with these guys if you didn't have to?"

Mal pointed to Stephanelli as if he were a dog.

"Chase Walker out of here," he ordered, then pointed at me. "Get 'em boy. Sic!"

Stephanelli gave me a crooked look, as if to let me know that what he was about to do was because he didn't have a choice. Then he lunged at me, hands first. I grabbed his arms but I was already falling backwards and with him diving forward we both went over Mike and did a somersault out the door.

I let go of him as I fell and tried to flip around in mid-air but didn't make it all the way. I hit hard on my left shoulder and folded over onto my back. I wasn't unconscious but the wind was knocked out of me. I lay dead-still, looking up at the twins, who were on all fours and leaning out the Box like two pit bulls.

Somewhere to my right I heard Stephanelli moaning. "I think I broke my arm," he whimpered. "Help me."

I pulled myself up onto my knees. I looked over at him. He was pawing the ground in pain. His other arm was folded over between the wrist and elbow.

"You're dead, Walker," Mike said. "We're calling the preacher and telling him everything. Everyone is going to know what a snitch you are."

"Oh, don't be so hard on him," Mal pleaded. "After all, there are going to be a lot of people who think he's a hero."

"True," Mike said. "Very true."

"Look, forget about me and help him." I pointed to Stephanelli. "You better get a doctor."

"He's our business," Mal said. "Now beat it before I come down there."

I stood up and stumbled off between the trees. And then I ran. I had to get to the preacher boy's trailer before Mike and Mal got to him first.

I really didn't have a plan. Not a clever plan, that is. If I was clever I might have figured out a way to save the girls. But I wasn't that shrewd, so I just saved myself. I figured I'd tell him everything. I'd make the deal with him he had first offered me. If he left my name out of it, he could have the girls, and I could go back to just being some no-name guy walking down a path, instead of having become some guy running across town to save his own ass.

When I passed the church the graffiti had been painted over. The walls were solid white again. If only I could paint over what I said last night, I thought, and make it all go away. But it was too late for that.

I walked around back to the house trailer. There was a little neon cross in the window. A dried-up potted palm was off to one side of the steps. The younger brother was standing on the back edge of the field laying out small square patches of new sod over the sand. To one side was a big cube of sod which had been dropped off by a truck.

I held my breath and pressed the doorbell.

In a minute the preacher boy looked out the window, then cracked the door open. "Funny seeing you here," he said, half in fear.

"I'm not here to hit you," I said.

"Then come in. You're just in time to see what I've set up for Halloween." He opened the door all the way.

I followed him into a small kitchen. "I have a deal to make. I came here because I have some information for you. And I'll tell you. But you have to promise not to let anyone know I'm the snitch."

He shook his head in disbelief. "I had given up on you," he said, grinning. "I thought, well, I was wrong about you. Thought I had finally found a tough nut too hard to crack. But it's good to know you came around after all."

He stuck his hand out to shake. "Okay," he said. "Give me their names, and I'll forget all about yours."

I shook his hand. "Karen Spencer and Jennifer Owet," I said.

He repeated their names. "The man upstairs loves you for this," he said smoothly. "You are definitely on His *good* list. You should be proud of yourself."

"Well, I'm not," I replied.

"Suit yourself," he said. "I guess you're just a modest hero. Now follow me, I got something to show you."

He took me down the short hallway and into the living room. "This is our Halloween Haunted House exhibit. We bring kids in here every Halloween to show them what the devil does to mankind. Believe me, we save more souls here than at Lourdes."

I stepped in behind him. There were old, chipped mannequins outfitted in Salvation Army donations, committing all kinds of sins. One was leaning against the wall and drinking from a broken bottle of Jack Daniel's. Little drops of nail-polish blood dripped down his chin and neck. Another man was sitting in a torn up La-Z-Boy with a syringe held awkwardly against his porcelain arm. Another was smoking a joint. They were staged as in some perverse movie where the toys and stuffed animals come to life at night, only this was with store mannequins that come to life for a sin party. It was creeping me out. It must have really terrified little kids.

"Let me take you into the bathroom," he said excitedly. "I just this second got an idea I want to run by you."

I followed him into the next cramped room. He opened the bathroom door. The light bulb was red, so everything had a hellish glow to it. I stepped in behind him, onto the fluffy red carpet.

"Here's what I'm thinkin'," he said. He reached over and pulled the jungle-print shower curtain back. "I could get a couple of female mannequins and have them kissing each other in here."

I must have stood there in shock for some time. It must have been shock because I don't remember feeling or thinking anything in particular beyond just a total wall of shame for being the snitch and helping this kid.

"Are you all right?" he asked. "Hey!"

I nodded. "Look, don't do this to them. Leave them alone. They haven't done anything to hurt you or anyone. Why don't you just leave them alone."

"Impossible," he replied. "God sent me on a mission to cleanse that school and I'm not turning back until the job is complete."

I grabbed him and shoved him backwards. He tried to steady himself on the shower curtain but it ripped away and he fell into the tub. I raised my arm to hit him.

"I wouldn't do that," he warned me, "Judas."

I lowered my fist and began to walk away.

"You were so easy," he shouted behind me. I heard him scuttling around in the tub like a crab. Finally he pulled himself up and shot out the door. "As easy to turn as all the rest. Every time I clean out a school, I just approach the first wimpy guy I see and start in on him and before long he can't take the pressure and he caves in." He snapped his fingers. "That simple," he said. "So I get a punch in the head every now and again. Big deal.

The payoff is *awesome*. And the next time I come around I won't have to pressure you. I'll just ask with a 'please and thank you' and you'll snitch again."

I trotted through the small rooms, then out the door and down the drive. I was completely spooked by the haunted house and the preacher kid. But I was even more afraid of being known as the snitch. I just hoped he'd keep his word and keep my name out of it.

No. No. No.

On Monday morning the preacher boy knew I would be arriving on my desire line and when he saw me coming he lifted the bullhorn to his lips. He was dressed in his striped suit, his boots were polished and his hair slicked back. He was ready. This was his big day. And it had arrived just as he knew it would.

As I jumped down from the fence onto the dried-up grass I felt as though I were picking my way through a mine field. With each step I expected him to blast, *"And here is the snitch!"* *Snitch! Snitch! Snitch!* And I'd go up in smoke.

But no. He just watched me, tracked me. Just let me tiptoe by like a criminal escapee. I only glanced over at him once, and that's all he was looking for. Because our eyes met for an instant and he winked and nodded. I was working for him. That's what his wink said. It also said, Don't worry. A deal is a deal. Your ass is covered. I headed for the animal pens thinking, I might just get out of this easy. My only concern was Mike and Mal. I didn't know what they were up to. But I had gotten to the preacher boy first, and if I was lucky that's where it would end.

Without warning the preacher boy started up. I guess he didn't think I was walking fast enough, but once I heard the sound of his voice I picked up my pace.

"Karen," *Karen. Karen. Karen.* "Jennifer!" *Jennifer. Jennifer. Jennifer.* "Come on out of the closet and into God's house." *House. House. House.* "Homosexuality is a sin. And the Bible beckons you to 'repent, or ye shall perish.' You can't escape the wrath of God."

Even with the metal lab door closed behind me I could still hear his televangelist voice. Over and over he continued to call out their names, and invited them into the church to change their wicked, sinful ways. Then he'd remind them that "the wages of sin is death." And when he got no reaction from them, he started over again.

I busied myself with the animal cages. There were more baby pigs. I cleaned them. I fed them. And I left them to their fate. They'd have a more merciful ending than the pigs I was trying to save. On Sunday I had found two more dead pigs at the golf course. They were chewed apart pretty good by either dogs or raccoons. I figured it wouldn't be long before I found the other five.

After I finished I walked down the wide main hall of the school like any other kid. No more slouching, spitting, and heel dragging. That was all behind me. I just walked in a straight line and when I looked at people it no longer seemed to me that they were thinking, There goes the faggot. Just a few days ago they had been staring a hole at me, but that was over with too. Now that everyone knew who the real "perverts" were, I was out of the picture. Everything was going as planned.

Until I went into biology class.

Karen was draped over her lab table with her head face-down in her hands. That threw me. I didn't think she'd be in school. I figured she and Jennifer might take a few days off and let things blow over as they had said.

But she was waiting for me, and when she heard my seat scrape across the floor she raised her head up and looked directly at me. At some point she had been crying. Her eyes were red and puffy. But she wasn't crying when she said, "It was you, wasn't it?" It came out more as a statement than a question.

She had figured out it was me, but I had figured out how to get out of it. "I don't know what you're talking about," I replied.

"Did you tell that preacher kid about us?"

"No," I said.

"Are you sure? He was after you to do that."

"It wasn't me," I insisted, and then without even planning to say so, I said, "It was Mike and Mal. They told me about you and Jennifer."

"Figures," she said bitterly. Then very quickly she packed her books into her book bag and stood up.

But she still wasn't sure. "Was it you?" she asked again.

"No," I replied.

She walked down the aisle toward Mr. Harvey. Every kid in the class was staring a hole in her. Everyone knew about her and Jennifer. And as she walked, I could imagine the other kids thinking, That's a dyke walk. And when she crossed her arms across her breasts, I imagined they thought, That's a dyke pose. And when she whispered something to Mr. Harvey, I could hear them thinking, That's a dyke lisp. But not one of them looked at me. My comfort zone had returned, but only on the outside. I wasn't too comfortable inside.

Mr. Harvey and Karen stepped out into the hallway. In a minute, only he returned. He picked up where he left off and I paid more attention to him than I had all year long.

I figured I'd never see her again. That it was over. That she'd walked out the door and would just keep going. Maybe she'd transfer to another school, or quit altogether. But on Tuesday she was back, sitting tensely in her chair, eyes straight ahead, elbows on the desk, with her hands holding up her head. The only thing I could think of when I saw her was a tuning fork, that someone had taken her and slapped her against the edge of a desk and set her in her seat and she was all stiff and vibrating at a pitch that could only be painful.

I kept glancing at her, furtively, as if I were cheating. I was looking at her face when she turned to me.

"Stop staring at me," she said. "If you want to know why I look like shit I'll tell you."

"Why?" I asked.

"He came to my house last night," she said. "That kid and his dad came in a truck with loudspeakers. They parked out in the street and called me every name in the book."

Even in class, as we were sitting there, I thought I could hear him. Or it could just have been his voice that I had heard so loud and so often ringing in my head.

"The good news is," she said, "my dad is a cop, so we called him and he came and chased them off. But they went over to Jennifer's house, until my dad chased them off there as well.

"The bad news is my dad now wants to know why I'm being called a dyke. Not to mention my mom, my brother and sister, Jennifer's family, and all the neighbors in a ten-block radius.

"Do you know why I'm telling you this?" she asked.

"Not really," I said.

"Because I want to know how you got him to stop harassing you."

"I punched him," I said. "And I threatened him until he gave up on me. You've got to crush him like a bug."

"Well, he's not giving up on us," she said.

Then rat someone out, I thought to myself. Pass the buck. Make a deal. Feed him a bigger fish.

"He'll give up," I said. "Your dad can scare him off."

"My dad is scaring me off," she said. "I'm not afraid of that little preacher creep. It's what trouble he's making that scares me most."

"Well, good luck," I said lamely.

She didn't come to school on Wednesday. The preacher boy knew it, too, and stayed inside his trailer. But he didn't have to say another word. He had gotten the ball rolling and the kids at school picked up where he left off. It seemed that wherever I was I could hear the girls being talked about. My duck pond was now the Dyke Pond. And the jokes were on everyone's lips.

How many dykes does it take to screw in a light-bulb? . . .

Did you hear about the little Dutch Boy who stuck his finger in the dyke? . . .

What do you get when you put two lesbians in a blender? . . .

.   .   .

I remembered overhearing Karen and Jennifer talking of a public hell, and now it had arrived. But the abuse from the preacher boy and what was going on in the school must have been only a small part of their hell. I tried to imagine their lives outside school. Bitter encounters at home with their families; being forbidden to ever see each other again; plans to transfer them to other schools; the hastily scheduled meetings with family ministers, or psychiatrists. I could think it all through, could see what was happening to them right in front of me, but I didn't feel it, didn't want to. I just kept my distance and studied them, safe but uncomfortable in my comfort zone.

On Thursday she still wasn't in biology. After Mrs. German's literature class, I dashed down the hall and out the door. I circled around to the back of the school and crossed the gym field. The preacher boy was nowhere in sight. After I hopped over the gate and started up the path, the white van with the roof speakers slowly passed by. The preacher dad with the slicked-down hair was driving. When he saw me he smiled broadly and gave me the thumbs-up.

I waved back with my bandaged hand. He slowed down but I veered off and kept going. I didn't want anything to do with him.

"*Hey!*" he yelled over the loudspeakers. "*I just want to talk with you.*"

I started to run.

"I just want to shake the hand of God's soldier!"

I kept going. I wasn't one of God's soldiers. And I had already shaken one hand and as far as I was concerned I had made a pact with the devil. He broadcast a few more things but I wasn't listening, and before long I was out of earshot.

When I arrived at the pond I pushed my hair back and sat down. I brought a book with me and read. The pond was mine again. Just me sitting there, reading, looking across at the ducks, and up into the cathedral of hissing trees. When I lowered my book and looked into the water I did not see someone beautiful. I was no Narcissus. Instead, I was repulsed by the reflection. I closed my eyes, but my mind was swirling inside just like the pond when the shafts of light cut through the gaps in the trees and shine deep into the water and expose something dark from down below.

I did not want any more secrets. But one more was thrust upon me. It was well after sundown and dark enough to not notice me, but light enough to see me, if you knew what you were looking at. I was sitting there in plain sight when Karen and Jennifer crashed through the bushes.

At first I thought they had tracked me down and had come to get me. But they didn't see me, and I didn't budge. I just slipped right back into watching them as I had always done.

Everything started quickly, like a film in fast forward, then gradually tapered down to slow motion and stopped for good. I know this because I have it fully memorized. I have had to ask myself many times if I saw correctly what happened.

First they kissed.

Then it was Jennifer who said, "Hurry. I don't want to think about it."

Karen reached into her bag and pulled out her father's police revolver.

At that moment, I could have stepped forward and changed everything. But I didn't. I thought if she saw me she'd shoot me, because if I were her I would have shot me.

Karen raised the gun up to Jennifer's head and Jennifer placed her own hand over the top of the cylinder to steady the barrel. Then they whispered something I couldn't make out.

In my mind I could draw a continuous line from my eyes spying on them to my brain, to my tongue speaking the secret in the Box, to a line passing into Mal's head, into his brain, coiling into his thoughts, and out his mouth and tongue, back to me, to the preacher boy, and that line looped from tongue to tongue, student to stu-

dent and now ran through Karen's heart to her shoulder
down her arm and into her hand, and when I tried to
snap the line it was too late, and her finger tightened and
she fired that first bullet directly into Jennifer's head.

The ducks scattered into the air. Jennifer slammed
against the tree, bounced back at Karen, and then col-
lapsed.

I flinched and by the time I stood up I saw the muz-
zle flash and heard the second shot. Karen's head
snapped back as she left her feet for a moment, before
she went down as hard as if she had fallen from the sky.

I ran. Ran like those boys who left their friend in the
pond to fight off the snakes. I knew they were both dead,
lying there against the side of the tree with the plastic
flowers.

But I was wrong. Karen was alive.

Last Man Out

Six months later Karen returned to school. Or, I should say, she was sent back as part of her rehabilitation, or maybe it was part of her therapy to come look me up. Whatever. One day I walked into biology class and Mr. Harvey had assigned her the same seat she had before, the one that had stayed vacant all the time she was gone, the one next to me. It was as if he had arranged a special science experiment, put the two of us in a cage, while he and the entire class stared down at us, waiting for something to happen.

Something *was* happening. But it was all inside me, buzzing, where no one could see it. My comfort zone was totally blown out. I kept thinking over and over, in the tiniest inner voice, as if my thoughts might be overheard, that I would not give up the new secret I had kept since the shooting. I hadn't told the police what I knew, and I wouldn't tell her. The more it ached to be let loose, the deeper I pushed it down, parked it in the back of my brain where it could pace back and forth until it wore itself out.

I discovered the secret two days after the shooting, when I read the newspaper story about the girls. I knew something was off immediately when I saw that they had labeled it ATTEMPTED MURDER–SUICIDE, and not MURDER–ATTEMPTED SUICIDE.

After I ran from the duck pond I put in an anonymous phone call to 911 from the U-Tote-Em. When the paramedics arrived they found Karen unconscious. According to the article, the shot fired at Karen's head was off-center and just glanced off her skull and knocked her out. After she was revived the next day, she stated that Jennifer shot her first, and she assumed that, while she was unconscious, Jennifer must have turned the gun on herself, and the gun must have dropped into the water. That's all she claimed to know. She was very steady about the whole thing.

The police bought her story, plus she was a cop's daughter, which had to help. They figured Karen was telling the truth because suicide notes written by both girls were left behind. The police never found the gun. I did not hear or see it land in the pond, but it must have. Police sent divers into the water. And, as before, when they had searched for that boy's body, they couldn't get to the bottom.

I knew Karen lied in order to save herself. That didn't bother me. Jennifer was dead and nothing could be done about it. But it left me as the only other person who knew what had really happened that night. And I wanted nothing to do with another secret.

Once Karen's wound healed she was sent away to a clinic upstate, and I figured I'd never see her again. I could just drop the secret into the pond and let it sink to the bottom, where it belonged.

A few days after the funeral I was changing classes when Mal caught up to me from behind. He spun me around and scared the crap out of me. He smiled and said, "Nice going, killer. I didn't think you had the balls." Then he gave me a buddy punch on the shoulder.

I didn't know what to say.

"Come visit us anytime," he said. "You know where we live."

But I didn't go back to the Box. I figured we'd just meet up in hell. In a strange way, the preacher boy was the only one I had to talk about it with. I should have hated him, but somehow I just didn't have any anger left in me. I felt numb, and I wondered how he *really* felt now that he could see the fruit of his labor.

One evening I walked over there to talk with him but they had pulled out of town. The beautiful church had already been unbolted from its foundation and trucked away. I figured they'd set up someplace else where they could shake down old folks, hunt homosexuals, burn books, stir up trouble, and maybe make a buck, then flee like gypsies being chased out of town once a mob has turned on them.

They must have fled pretty quickly because they left behind their Halloween house trailer. Kids had already broken in and thrown all the stuff outside. The sinning mannequins were stacked up in a pile out back on the dead sod. I found the girls among them. They wore name tags stuck to their shoulders. HELLO, MY NAME IS JEN-NIFER. HELLO, MY NAME IS KAREN. Their voices sounded in my ear like the robotic voices of dolls when you pull their neck cord and they speak in broken phrases.

There was another mannequin lying next to them, with shiny painted hair and smily teeth. Gold-foil candy coins were glued to his hand. The chocolate had melted out and run down his fingers like bloodstains from a stig-mata. Ants were running back and forth, still trying to pinch off another bite. And on his shoulder there was a name tag. HELLO, MY NAME IS WALKER. That jolted me. I reached down and tried to peel it off, but it wouldn't un-stick. I picked up a rock and scratched over it until you couldn't tell. Then I ran off before anyone saw me.

Of course I continued with school. I buckled down and studied and did my own work, and really, it didn't take long until I was back in a routine. For the school, the shooting just blended in with the rest of the usual scandals.

That is, until the moment Karen showed up in biology class. After I took my seat next to her I sat there wondering what I should say or do. Of course nothing came to mind except that I knew she was the shooter, knew she pulled the trigger, knew it must have been awful to believe you're totally blown away, dead gone, then suddenly you open your eyes and you're back where you started, only with the death of a person you love on your hands.

She looked over at me. It was the most broken look on a human face I had ever seen. It wasn't as if she were going to collapse into tears. It wasn't a sad look. It was as if she had been hollowed out, that what was once vital in her was gone, that she was a person without a personality, without character. As if someone had jabbed her in the chest with a giant syringe and just sucked the life right out of her.

Mr. Harvey chattered on about who knows what. He could have been reading the *Penthouse Forum* letters out loud and I wouldn't have paid attention. I was totally consumed with her sitting next to me, and my mind was just playing the shooting scene over and over until she removed a small piece of paper from her notebook and began to write. Then, just as before, as if I was cheating off her test, I slowly glanced at the paper.

They want me to speak with you, she wrote. *It's part of my therapy.*

She passed me the paper. It's not part of my therapy, I thought, but instead wrote, *What do you want to talk about?* I paused a moment and slid it toward her. My hand was shaking.

What really happened.

She stared at me as I read. It was eerie, really, that her face wouldn't change. It was just set, as though it had been an elaborate doll's face with dozens of small moving parts, but it had been broken and was now all glued together and the moving parts were rigidly fixed.

Sure, I wrote.

I'll meet you at the pond, she replied. *Tonight. Nine o'clock.*

I nodded.

I arrived early and knelt down behind the boxwood bushes on the other side of the water.

When you spy on anyone, peek in windows, watch someone from across a room, you become a secret audience, and they become a secret theater. When Karen arrived I was hidden. Her every move seemed theatrical, seemed to have a meaning I was supposed to guess at. And it was my guess that she had a gun. I figured she was going to blow me away and this time properly finish herself off. I watched her more intently than when she was naked. But I didn't see a gun.

Instead, she acted as if she were waiting for Jennifer to show up. She removed a wool camp blanket from a canvas tote and spread it between the big tree and the edge of the pond. She crawled across the blanket, carefully smoothing the surface with her hands, seeking out the sharp spots as she worked, occasionally lifting the flap and removing a rock or branch. When she finished, she withdrew two votive candles and lit them at the base of the tree. The flames, shining through the blue glass, cast a murky shadow across the rough bark. When her face entered the circle of light, it was not soft, but somber. Her mouth was a tight line over the cup of her chin. After a few minutes, I could smell the wax.

She sat with her back to the tree, then almost immediately sat up again. The wind gusted, and for a moment the rustling leaves could be mistaken for someone pushing through the bushes, as if Jennifer were about to arrive, or me.

Then she said, "Come on out, Walker. I know you're hiding in the bushes."

I stepped out. "I just got here," I said.

She stood up. "One of the reasons I came back is so you would know exactly what I know, and I could find out what you know."

"I think I know enough already," I said. "I know more than I want to know."

"Do you know I spoke to Mike and Mal and they told me everything? Do you know I even tracked down the preacher kid? I know you were the one with the big mouth. Now, do you have anything more to say?"

I looked at her head where I imagined the bullet had struck. Then I looked down at her hands to make sure they were empty.

"You must know you got away with murder," she said harshly.

"Me?" I replied. "Murder? Did I murder anyone? I don't think so."

"What's really important is that you and I know who really killed her. Don't you, Walker? Think about it," she said.

"I don't have to," I replied. "I was right here the night it happened." I pointed to where I had been sitting. "I saw it all. You were the shooter. I'm the one who called the cops. I could have told them who really killed her."

If she was surprised by this information, she didn't show it. "It doesn't matter anymore what the police know or don't know," she snapped back. "That part's over with. I've had six months to think about this. I wish to God I hadn't pulled the trigger. I wish I could have just laughed in that preacher boy's face instead of letting him get me. But you got it worse than me. You're the one who served us up. You gave him just what he wanted."

"It wasn't me," I said, thinking that I had already said that.

"Well, thanks for coming out tonight," she said bitterly, and stepped away. "Thanks for nothing."

"Hey, nobody had to hold a gun to my head," I lashed out.

She turned around and looked me directly in the eye. "That's just what Mal said about you," she replied. "Nobody had to hold a gun to your head." Then she turned on her flashlight and cut between the trees, leaving behind the blanket and candles. I stood there and watched her tramp down a path through the tall grass, the slash of her light leading the way. The cattails had gone to seed and drifted across the fairway like balls of cotton. And then she was gone.

And I was standing there looking down into the pond. The candle lights reflected like angel wings across the shiny surface. And I froze there, just staring, like I do, gazing into the water as though hypnotized. And I knew I was feeling something that had not yet been put into words. I hadn't showed up to say vicious things. I had wanted to apologize. I wanted to say I was sorry. But that's not what came out. Whatever happened to the girls was over with for me. But whatever was pacing back and forth in the dark part of my soul was still stirring around, was still looking for trouble. I turned and walked away, down my desire line.

I wondered what it was like to be the last person to leave Palenque, Machu Picchu, or Angkor Wat. It must have been every man for himself. At the end, the last person didn't die there. He died running away.